NATALIE

In the Shadow of the Swastika

ANTOINETTE CONSTABLE

Vésinet Books

NATALIE

In the Shadow of the Swastika

Published by Vésinet Books

ISBN 978-1-7331819-4-5

Cover and text design: Jim Shubin, BookAlchemist.net
Author photo: Laurie McAndish King

To all children whose lives
have been upended by a war

Contents

1940

Chapter 1

Papa

Papa's room was empty. His mattress bare, his clothes, his books, his pencils and drawing pads all gone, only his photo of the ship he'd served on, *Le Strasbourg*, hung on the wall. Eight-year-old Natalie stood rooted, three feet inside his room. On this special day, had the Germans grabbed him?

Everyone knew that the Germans took over large homes to lodge their officers. Two weeks ago, a mean-looking man in a gray uniform swollen at the thighs above shiny boots, with a gun on his belt, had run up the stairs, two at a time, kicking each door open on the landing until he found Papa in bed, coughing into that horrible metal cup with a lid, spitting out red foam. The officer had turned on his heels and rushed out, rubbing the index finger of one hand with the index finger of the other hand fast. Then he did the same thing with the other hand as if they were splattered in stink. After the officer left, Maman said, "It's a blessing they're so afraid of germs."

Natalie and her sisters—Hélène, fourteen, and Liliane, nick-named Lilla, almost five years old—were only allowed to visit Papa five minutes each day from the threshold of his room. They were forbidden to kiss him, or hug him, or touch anything of his. How could five minutes be enough? Natalie had so much to tell him.

"Why is Papa gone? Did the German officer come back? Where is Maman?" Natalie asked Hélène anxiously as they both faced Papa's empty room.

Hélène shrugged. "I don't know. I found a note on the table. Maman wrote that I'm in charge until she returns."

Both Papa and Maman were gone! Natalie refused to believe it. "No," she shouted. "It's not true! It's Maman's birthday today. We will sing 'Joyeux Anniversaire' by Papa's door, and I have a present for Maman!" She had saved twelve tiny wild strawberries she'd found in the shady garden.

Hélène took her by the arm and dragged her downstairs. "Last week, I heard Maman talking on the phone," she whispered.

"What does the stupid phone have to do with Papa?" Natalie demanded. She scowled at Hélène. "And where is Lilla?'

"With Maman."

Natalie felt cold with disappointment. She didn't know what was worse: that Papa had left without saying goodbye, or that he wasn't home for Maman's special day. His room was empty. The birthday and the singing and the presents were forgotten, as if Maman didn't exist, as if her birthday had never been. Natalie felt tears coming.

No, she wouldn't cry. She raised her head to prevent her tears from leaking out. She crossed her third finger over her index finger on both hands. Rosie, her best friend, had told her it brought luck. Hélène took her to her room. They sat on Natalie's bed. Hélène put an arm around Natalie's shoulders. To console her, Hélène brought out of her pocket a photo of Papa from a few years ago. He stood straight and smiling by a white ship, very smart in his French Navy officer's uniform with gold buttons. She said, "For you, Nat."

Hot tears ran down Natalie's face. She blew her nose and kissed her photo. How could they live without Papa?

Hélène murmured, "I heard Maman discussing on the phone when Papa could be taken in."

Natalie asked, "Taken where?"

"To the hospital. I don't know what the other person said."

There was nothing to do but wait for Maman to return. Natalie didn't even bother to open her school bag to glance at her homework. When, hours later, Maman came home with Liliane, she called the girls into the living room. It must be serious, Natalie thought, walking in reluctantly. She asked, "What about your birthday, Maman?"

They had made birthday cards for her. Hélène, of course, had made the best one. It showed Maman, all in green, arm in arm with Papa, both smiling in front of their two-story yellow millstone house. She'd managed to show its pink and silver tinges and the glass awning gleaming over the eight front steps. Lilla's card was fine too because Hélène had helped her. Natalie had done her best, drawing a house over a large cake, but it wasn't very good.

"I'll enjoy no birthday until the war is over," said Maman. "From now on, the three of you must behave at all times as if Papa were home, since, if he's done nothing else, he's kept the Germans away from us. You must be extremely careful who you play with and what you confide in others," Maman continued, wagging a finger at Natalie. "Do not trust anyone, because if you do, you'll put all of us in danger. Do you understand?"

Natalie was horrified. There was a problem. Yesterday she had told her best friend, Rose, that Maman was Jewish. Rose and Natalie were best friends. Because they shared a birth date, they pretended to be twins brought up in different homes, sometimes exchanging their cardigans, reading the same books, chatting endlessly, even in class. Rose's father was an Englishman who traveled to England for his job, so he was often gone. Georgette, a nosy new girl in her class, who lived seven blocks away on the same street, kept running after her and Rosie, reaching Rose to pull her long blond hair, wanting to know what they were talking about. They didn't tell her, but Natalie thought that perhaps Georgette had heard.

What if the German officer found out that Papa was away? Would he return to throw Maman, Hélène, Lilla and herself out? Where would they go? Maman's own family had left long ago, but where? Since Maman had quarreled with Papa's mother, they no longer visited each other. That was a big problem. Natalie bit her nails.

At home, in the following weeks, with Papa gone, they didn't laugh anymore and didn't want to play. Maman was often in a bad mood. Lilla became a crybaby clinging to Maman. Then, there was Hélène who was very nice sometimes, explaining difficult things. But now Hélène sulked and spent her time practicing the same sad, boring piano piece instead of doing her chores. "Für Elise" was drawn out enough to make anyone cry. Because that man Beethoven had written such awful music, she, Natalie, must peel potatoes when they managed to get some, and she must do the ironing instead of Hélène, or Maman became very angry. Sometimes Hélène said "thank you," but only sometimes. When Natalie complained, Maman said, "Can't you girls ever take the initiative and simply do what needs to be done?"

At bedtime during those early weeks of Papa's absence, Natalie's nose twitched again as when tears came. No, she wouldn't cry. Since Maman said that her girls must take initiative, she would. She had an idea. She sniffed and sat up, crossing her fingers for luck. All she had to do was to find Papa and convince him to come home.

1941

Chapter 2

Germans in Town

Papa had left two months after the Germans occupied their town, Le Vésinet, a western suburb of Paris. After months spent indoors, Natalie ventured into the garden on her tenth birthday. The second chestnut tree from in the gate, close to the ivy-covered fence, offered a lower branch from which she hoisted herself up along the trunk to her observation post. From behind the fan-like leaves, she saw a truck out of which popped dull gray-green puppet-like figures.

At the intersection, a German in uniform gave a staccato speech, gesticulating toward five soldiers. He looked like the German officer with two guns who'd insisted on inspecting the house, refusing to believe that Papa was sick in bed upstairs. Natalie wondered how the Germans could understand each other. She watched two soldiers swiveling on their heels. Three others measured the sidewalk and drew crosses on the street with chalk.

Craning her neck, Natalie tried to guess their plan. Over her ear, one of her braids came undone. The German shouting orders in the middle of the street rubbed his gloved hands together, chin on his chest. The corners of his mouth were down so that he looked disgusted, though there was nothing disgusting to see. Then, looking up toward her, he smiled.

Natalie was alive with surprise. He'd known she was in

her tree. Could he read her thoughts through the leaves and see she was afraid? She hugged the scratchy bark, holding her breath, unable to cross her fingers for luck. She had not hidden herself well enough.

The German officer walked to the edge of the sidewalk and winked. He raised his palm, offering Natalie her ribbon still knotted like a yellow bowtie. Inside his German hand, Natalie saw nothing but a pale satin moth that couldn't possibly be her ribbon. She didn't move. The German placed the moth-ribbon on the gatepost, turned to the men in gray-green cloth caps chalking the trees and the sidewalks, and jotted things in his notebook.

The Germans looked just like other men. Natalie had not expected that. Street posters depicted them as raving, green-faced monsters that strangled babies and plunged curved swords into the tummies of grimacing women unable to run away. She didn't know what to think.

In the morning, Natalie found two trees on the sidewalk on either side of the gate reduced to stumps. Her chestnut tree had been chopped down, and it was her own fault since the German officer had seen her in it. The Germans not only wanted more homes for their officers, they wanted to easily check the comings and goings on the streets. Soon there would be no more trees, at least that is what the friendly neighborhood policeman told Maman.

1942

Chapter 3

Nothing Is the Same

Four months later, Natalie sat next to Hélène who struggled with her high school Latin homework spread over the dining room table. Natalie looked up the Latin words for Hélène in a special dictionary. She read the French texts Hélène must translate. The Romans were cruel. They spent their time in battles, massacres, setting homes on fire and torturing animals and people. Natalie promised herself never to learn Latin. She gazed at the newspaper spread on the oilcloth table cover, under a handful of green beans from the garden. "Traitors will be shot on sight," stated the bold headline. "Hélène," she asked, "are the Germans worse than the Romans?"

Tongue sticking out from the corner of her mouth, Hélène wasn't busy with her Latin. She was drawing a peacock. She spent much time drawing, and she was very good at it. Natalie wished she too were good at something valuable. "Do you have to interrupt when I do something difficult?" Hélène fumed. "Go learn your history lesson!"

Natalie was tired of reading about the Louis Kings of France. There were too many. She went to the kitchen where Maman was wearing a white apron as she made jelly for the winter. She had been given a crate of red currants and was stirring them as they simmered in a large cauldron. Soon she would spoon samples into saucers and there would be pink froth over samples of jelly for the girls to taste. Natalie wanted to ask where Papa had gone. But first, she must tell Maman about mean Georgette. "Georgette keeps calling me names, Maman."

Georgette and her parents were newcomers to a gaudy yellow villa, eight blocks away. "Horrid names, Maman," she continued.

"For instance?" Maman stirred the bubbles without looking up.

"She called me *Youpine, une sale juive*. A *Yid*. A dirty Jew. Tell her, Maman, tell her I'm not dirty and I'm not a Jew."

"Her father works at the town hall. He has access to all residents' files." Maman was stirring slowly against a resistance inside the wide copper pot.

"*Mais*, Maman, it's a lie, isn't it?"

"The Germans believe that children take after their father, not their mother. Your father is a Protestant, so the Germans will not consider you as Jewish children. I became a Protestant at sixteen. So to them, you aren't a Jew. Anyway, there's nothing to be ashamed of." Maman frowned. "Avoid arguments with Georgette, especially about whether or not you're Jewish, Natalie. Don't think about it."

Natalie blinked. She didn't understand what Maman had said. Either something was true, or it wasn't. Why not talk about it if there was nothing wrong? And how was she not to think about something? That was hard. There was a nasty German, worse than an ogre, who liked to kill people. She would try not to think about Mr. Gestapo, but it wasn't going to be easy. Nothing made sense. Nothing was the same. Even Le Vésinet was hard to recognize. The town had changed. Stern soldiers in strange gray uniforms marched on the sidewalks as if no one else walked there so that people must step into the street to let them pass, or be knocked down.

The German troops paraded everywhere. At the shops, they marched to the head of long lines to be served first. They poked about the school grounds and draped the front of the buildings they confiscated with enormous red flags with a crooked black cross in the middle.

Natalie made her way back to the garden. She drew the mail from the mailbox and found in it a postcard addressed to her from Papa. Without showing it to anyone, she read its simple message, kissed her card, and ran upstairs to hide it under the lining of her top drawer. Before slipping it in, she looked for an address, which she didn't find.

Chapter 4

Star of David

One day in June Maman had to wear the Star of David.

"Why?" the girls asked, from the foot of the stairs.

"It's a new German law. Unless you can prove that for three generations there are no Jews among your ancestors, you must." Maman was polishing the dark wood of the banister.

Hélène touched her forehead. "Say you don't know who they were, that you were adopted," she insisted.

"That counts as being Jewish." Maman's face was red, perhaps from rubbing the banister so hard.

"Will you wear it all the time?" Lilla asked. "To the market and the bread line and the butcher's?" She, too, had received a card from Papa, which she carried everywhere so that it already looked grubby.

"To the market, to the bread line and the butcher. To the milk line, the church, the post office. Everywhere." Maman didn't look up. When she stopped polishing, with her back turned, she said, "I count on you, children, to remind me to wear it. Will you?"

"I won't," Natalie cried, making her good luck sign with the fingers of both hands. "I'll never remind you. At school they say to spit on Jews. What if somebody did that to you?"

Maman ignored her outburst. She said, "From now on, I must go every day to the police station to sign my name. So you see, I must remember." She fetched her sewing kit.

"Maman?"

"What is it?" Maman placed a few pins on the left lapel of her coat ready to sew a Star of David on it.

"May I hold it?" Natalie asked. If Papa had been there, he would have known what to do.

Maman let her hold the circle of yellow cloth, about three inches in diameter, showing a six-pointed star. Inside the black outline, a word in spiky letters sat like a black spider: *Juif*. "Jew," Natalie said, and held it far from her, as if it had claws. Maman took it back.

Another law ordered Jews to shop only between 1 p.m. and 3 p.m. But the shops were closed for lunch until 3 p.m. They were open until 7 p.m. at night, so Hélène and Natalie began shopping for Maman when they weren't at school, taking their indispensable ration cards along with net bags. Eyes averted, Natalie pretended not to see the Star of David armbands of shame on old men, skinny boys and girls, and pale women who wore theirs on jackets and coats. What Maman needed was often sold out, or the girls were sold smaller portions of cheese or sugar than their rations allowed, though they still must relinquish coupons to the shopkeepers and pay full price.

Natalie tried to wash Maman's dress with the star to erase it. She hung it in the back garden to dry. Like water paints in the rain, the colors ran and the dress was ruined. Maman was furious. From then on, she wore her star sewn on a short grey shawl. When she was home, Maman left the shawl on the banister so that the children knew as soon as they walked in whether she was in.

Natalie saw that she had been wrong to try to wash the star away. That was impossible. Why did she never have really good ideas?

Not long after that, Hélène's application for Camp Fire Girls was declined. Scouting was forbidden to Jews. The church lady said she was so sorry, but she could not afford to be labeled a Jew sympathizer. Weeks earlier, Hélène's piano teacher had refused to give her lessons because she was afraid to be seen entering a Jewish home. Maman sold their piano to a neighbor for three bags of coal. He came with his wife and a friend to pull and push the piano out of the house, lifting it over the gravel of the driveway till they reached the street.

Maman turned to Natalie. "I never liked that piano. We'll get a better one when the war is over. Then you can have lessons." Natalie didn't believe that Maman disliked the piano because she had tears in her eyes. Now there was too much room in the living room, even after she helped Maman move arm-chairs toward the window and rearrange the rugs.

In addition to the star problem, there were many words Natalie overheard in adult conversations. They seemed dangerous, like swear words, not to be pronounced at home—*Komandantur, Ausweiss, Abwher,* demarcation line, requisition—all mixed with the names of French towns like Cannes, Nice and Casablanca. At night, she fell asleep among the dangerous swear words that spilled over a map of France and its colonies. Natalie badly wanted to find Papa to tell him how much they needed him at home, but though she'd overheard his hospital address in Paris, she knew letters took a long time, and she needed a stamp. Besides, after writing to tell Papa she was coming, she also would need to buy a train ticket to Paris and a bus ticket to his hospital. She had only two francs in her china piggybank. It wasn't enough. She planned to ask Hélène for help, but she must only ask when Hélène was in a good mood. In the meantime, she must help Maman. She sorted the sheets and pillowslips to be washed together with blouses and napkins so they would be ready for the washing machine that sat in the shack at the back of the house.

One night, Natalie hid Maman's shawl under her pillow. She used Maman's nail scissors to unstitch the star. The best place to crush that black spider on the star was between her blotter and her white scribbled-on blotting paper. Natalie was pleased to have found a way to make the star problem go away. But in the morning, Maman rushed about looking for the star. When she eventually found it, she shouted at Natalie that she was nothing but trouble and ordered her to her room. Perhaps Maman was upset because she had fewer and fewer visitors. In bed that night, Natalie moped and dreamt of saving Maman from the many unfair rules of the Germans and the government. In the morning, she couldn't remember what bravery had led her, a few hours before, to try to solve the black spider problem and win Maman's love.

In addition to the star problem, there were more new words Natalie overheard in adult conversations, words she had never heard before. "What does it mean, Aryanization, *Feldgrau, couvre-feu, bayonette,* black market, *passer la ligne?*" she asked Hélène.

"Nothing to do with us, Nat. It's about the war and soldiers, that's all," Hélène said.

Natalie knew Hélène was holding something—or many things—back. Hélène was stubborn, so it did no good to insist. Better wait till she volunteered.

When Hélène received a second postcard from Papa, Natalie asked, "Hélène, do you want to go and see Papa in Paris?"

"I went once with Maman," Hélène admitted. "The hospital people wouldn't let me into his room. Don't you try anything stupid."

Natalie was very upset that Maman had taken Hélène to see Papa without her. In the bathroom, while brushing her teeth, she tried to think of someone who would go to see Papa with her. She didn't come up with anyone, except perhaps Grand-Maman who lived far away. Should she phone? But Maman would notice the phone call on the bill and be angry because she didn't like Grand-Maman. She wondered how much it would cost for a phone call to Versailles if she called from her friend Rosie's home?

Long trips, phones—Natalie had way too many problems. The only good thing was that Lilla had been happy to exchange her fifty centimes piece for Natalie's two coins of ten centimes, because she believed that more coins meant more money. Natalie had hugged Lilla and played with her a long time before dinner to thank her, but she still didn't have enough money for a train ticket from Le Vésinet to Paris and then on to Versailles. She decided simply to save and save, and one day she would be able to buy a ticket. Luckily she had found a single wrinkled franc bill stuck under a hedge near the market. She flattened it as much as she could and hid it with the rest of her coins, pushing the money through a crack in the corner of her double-bottom chest of drawers.

Chapter 5

Only Le Strasbourg is Left

Natalie's eleventh birthday had taken place in August, which seemed such a long time ago, since the trees were now bare. Soon it would be Christmas. From Versailles, Grand-Papa and Grand-Maman sent the sisters an invitation without mentioning Maman. Hélène put it into words at lunch. "Grand-Papa doesn't like Jews. He must be afraid of them."

No one answered.

On Christmas day, bundled up against the cold, Maman and her three girls took two trains to Versailles. They had to walk from the station to Grand-Papa's and Grand-Maman's villa instead of taking a pedicab because Maman wasn't allowed to ride in a rickshaw. Pedicabs looked like such fun. People used them because taxis and buses had been left to rust for lack of gasoline. A man pedaled a bike with a box large enough to seat two, made of wicker or wood planks, attached to the back. At the villa, instead of dinner, tea had been prepared with cookies and an apple tart because Maman, as a Jew, wasn't allowed in the streets after dark. Nobody mentioned it.

At tea, Grand-Maman spoke of people called Free Masons, who, like the Jews, were accused by the Germans of causing the war. Maman was quiet. Natalie heard more frightening words: cyanide, mass rounding-ups, the sinking of the fleet, Rommel. Grand-Maman declared, "With our dear Marshall Pétain at the helm, all will turn out for the best. What we need is patience! I don't think that's your strong suit, Noémi."

Maman shook her head and changed the subject. "I heard our fleet was destroyed last month by the British, every ship except perhaps *Le Strasbourg,* someone said." Papa had served on *Le Strasbourg* before becoming sick, Natalie remembered with a shudder.

Grand-Maman fanned herself with her hand as if to blow away what Maman was telling her.

"You're a young mother, Noémi. Your first duty is to look after your children. I don't see how listening to improbable reports—gossip, really—can achieve anything. It must be a mistake. Yes, if it's true, England must have made a mistake. That happens in wartime. There is probably little truth to the news anyway. You should rejoice in the fact that we managed to have Francis transferred to a hospital in Switzerland."

Switzerland? Natalie hadn't known that Papa was no longer in Paris. She promised herself to read everything she could about Switzerland. It sounded very far from France.

After tea, the maid drew the drapes shut. She turned off the electricity as soon as Grand-Papa lit the candles clipped to the branches on the Christmas tree. The sitting room was filled with a dreamy soft orange glow that made Natalie's heart beat faster. In the dark, she sought Hélène's hand, who gave Natalie's a reassuring squeeze. "I have something to tell you later," Hélène murmured.

"Tell me now!" Natalie begged.

Grand-Maman said, "Be quiet, children."

The maid turned the electricity on again and Grand-Maman played the piano. They listened to "Silent Night" and Papa's favorite, "Angels in the Countryside," while Grand-Papa arranged wrapped presents around the tree for them to take home. Natalie was sad because no one mentioned Papa. She crossed her third finger over her index finger, remembering

Maman's instructions that there were to be no "unpleasant incidents" during this visit.

Since no one was helping her understand the new words, as she said goodbye, Natalie asked, "Grand-Papa, what does *Maquis* mean?"

After a silence, he replied, "It's a sort of desert in Corsica. This is for you." He handed her a bag of presents.

"What's strychnine, Grand-Papa?" she persisted, standing in front of him.

"This is not the time for a vocabulary lesson, Natalie," he said, bushy eyebrows touching.

"Nobody wants to tell me. Is it because nobody knows?" she asked, a hand at her waist.

Grand-Papa was not pleased. "We invited you to share a lovely Christmas tea. Let's keep questions for another time. Now, let me hug your little sister goodbye," he added, opening his arms to Lilli.

Natalie insisted, "What about strychnine?" She had heard about strychnine. Someone said people resorted to it.

"It's a poison to kill rats," he said very fast. An eleven-year-old child shouldn't ask so many questions. Enough."

To kill rats? What did it have to do with people? Natalie thought of prisoners taken by the Germans being like rats in cages. Was that what happened in prisons? Were prisoners made to eat poison?

They returned home along empty streets before dark. Near the train station, in the waning light, they passed new large notices about three executions pasted onto bare walls. To prevent Lilla from seeing them, Maman put her hands over Lilla's eyes, asking her to guess the name of the street.

At home, as soon as the girls opened their presents, there was a power failure. In the dark, the house felt colder. Lilla hugged her box of dominoes, Hélène her bag of beads, ribbons and strings to make jewelry, which had come with a book of illustrations. Natalie dropped her book about the Baron of

Munchausen. She didn't want it because the baron was German, though the pictures on glossy paper were tempting. She'd read it later. Grand-Maman had also given her a blue cardigan with a yellow belt, her favorite colors.

Grand-Maman had given Maman a pot of strawberry jam and enough tapioca to make one dessert for them. Maman saved their daily milk rations for breakfast—a cup for each child. In the dark kitchen, using a candle, she boiled the tapioca in water for their dinner. She saved half the tapioca for another day.

"Frog's eggs, I tell you! It tastes just like frogs," Hélène whispered into Natalie's ear as they devoured the tapioca. Natalie wanted to ask when Hélène had eaten frog meat or eggs, but Maman was watching. They ate their frog's eggs in silence. At least, the strawberry jam on top tasted good. It wouldn't last long, because the pot was small.

After dinner, Hélène cleared the table. Natalie took the dictionary to her room. Now she understood "propaganda," "partisans," and "armistice," which meant both sides in a war agreed to stop fighting. She did not find "Aryanization" or "Gestapo," though she tried several times. If every country had its Gestapo, why was it not in the dictionary? She no longer believed it was someone's name. She hadn't found all the explanations she wanted, but the little she found was better than nothing. She undressed and put on two pairs of pajamas to keep warm. Then she walked into Hélène's room and sat on her bed. "You had something to tell me," she reminded Hélène, who was putting her hair in curlers.

"I did? What about?"

"We were talking about words I can't find."

"Oh, those words...*Maquis*? Well, it's where people who fight the Germans go to hide."

Natalie blinked. "In Corsica?"

"There's a *Maquis* in France as well. There are no roads into it and nothing much grows there."

Natalie nodded. "What's Aryanization?"

"A German plan to get rid of Jews."

"All of them?"

"That's why Maman must wear a star. And why she must hide sometimes."

Maman called from downstairs, "Enough visiting in each other's rooms, girls. I'll be up to kiss you good night in five minutes."

Natalie scurried to her own bed, still worrying about Corsica, strychnine, yellow stars and big frog-size puddles of tapioca. In bed at night, she dreamt of saving Maman from the unfair German rules, like having no right to a radio, to own a dog, to go to concerts or plays where Papa used to take her, or sit in cafes, restaurants, or parks, or even use public telephones, though with Papa's help, Natalie was sure she could find a way.

1943

Chapter 6

Getting an Idea

In February 1943 as Natalie was tracing a map of European countries, a power shortage interrupted her. Even with her nose close to the paper, she couldn't see where Germany ended and France started. Blackouts were hateful. Geography was hateful. The war was hateful. The Germans were hateful. She ran to the hall, grabbed Maman's shawl from the banister, came back into the dining room and stood on tiptoe to look taller.

In the dark, she volunteered, "I'll wear it for you, Maman."

Maman became as angry as if Natalie had screamed obscenities. "Don't you ever say such a thing!" she shouted.

"I am your daughter," Natalie insisted. Maman grabbed Natalie by her forearms and shook her. "You're nothing like me! And if you were, what would that prove? Yes, you're my daughter, but you're least like me. Believe me, you take after your father. You look like him. I'm reminded every day of my life!"

The door slammed behind Maman whose voice reverberated around the room and even the typewriter Maman was teaching herself to use vibrated in the darkness. Natalie didn't know what she'd done wrong, only that Maman didn't like her because she never did anything right.

She picked up the shawl and let it droop onto the banister. She wondered if Maman disliked her because she looked like Papa. Impossible. Maman loved Papa. That was why she'd married him. She had Hélène and Natalie and Lilla. Mostly Maman loved her, except she couldn't help it if she looked like Papa! Natalie went to see Hélène in her room at bedtime, planning to ask something easy first.

"What does it mean, black market?" she asked.

"That's how rich people buy all sorts of stuff we can't afford." Hélène spoke with her head hidden inside the dress she was taking off.

"Hélène, do I look like Papa?"

"You look like Papa, all right," Hélène answered in her petticoat, rummaging into a box of colored chalks.

"But I look like Maman too, *un petit peu,* a little bit?"

"Mmm. You have black hair like Maman, that's all. Your eyes are blue like Papa's. Want me to tell you who you look like?" Hélène climbed, shoeless, on a chair, drawing the animals of the Ark on the pink wallpaper of her room, above her bedside table. One monkey hung upside-down, his tail curling like a rope around a branch. The leopard she'd drawn yesterday had only one eye open. Hélène grinned. Natalie expected a joke. "You look like Papa's mother, that's who," she said, turning around. "What's more, Maman and Grand-Maman can't stand each other. I thought you knew. They hardly speak."

"Why? Because Maman is Jewish?"

"Figure it out. You'd better go to bed now, or we'll both be in trouble."

Natalie returned to Papa's study where she slept on the sofa because it was less cold than in her room under the roof. She'd heard about the Jewish shops on the elegant Champs-Elysées, in Paris, attacked, looted, their windows smashed by people who hated Jews. She felt very angry. Why didn't the French police stop the nasty people? It wasn't fair. And it wasn't fair that Maman liked her sisters better than her—all because she looked too much like Grand-Maman.

Then she had an idea. If at school in the morning she wrote the best composition, and was given a good grade, she would prove her worth. She would rise to the top; she would be the best, and Maman would be proud of her too.

Chapter 7

A Telephone Call

The situation for Jews was steadily worsening. Natalie heard plenty about what happened to Jews when they were caught. She heard it at home, in the streets, during raids when they ran to shelters, after curfew when she waited in long lines for provisions, and during recess when girls talked among themselves. It was too horrible. She must not think about Maman running to some secret place, trying to evade pursuers and hiding, not knowing when it would be safe for her to return home.

Food was scarce. Money was scarce. Maman had no money to buy gifts. For her birthday, Hélène had received a gold bracelet with a pencil attached by a little chain. It had been given to Maman at sixteen, to jot down the names of young men who wanted to polka or waltz with her at dances. Ahead of her twelfth birthday, Maman gave Natalie a little wooden box from her own dresser, telling her that Papa had made it during a summer in Switzerland when he was her age.

Natalie planned to save Papa's postcards in his felt-lined box with a hinged lid, though no postcards had come for any of them in a long time.

Late one Sunday afternoon during the summer, Natalie stood at the ironing board sprinkling water from a spray-top bottle onto clothes she lifted from the basket. Her twelfth birthday was coming soon, and she realized she was old enough to help Maman, who had lots of problems.

The phone rang. She tore along the passage to answer the

call before Hélène could rush down from her room. A man's voice spoke a few numbers and hung up without giving his name.

"Who was it?" Maman asked from the open bathroom door. She was brushing her long, blue-black hair.

"Some man. He said 'nine, sixty-one, twenty-two' and he hung up. What does it mean?"

Maman threw her hairbrush into a drawer. "I'll be back as soon as I can," she announced, and left without saying where she was going.

Would Maman come home before the curfew, or during the night? If she didn't return, how could they tell Madame Martineau, their old cleaning woman, who had no telephone? Madame Martineau was to hide them when she or Hélène arrived with Lilla. Natalie remembered fat Madame Martineau cleaning the house before Papa fell ill.

Lilla fell asleep on the sofa. On the coffee table last week's newspaper announced that on February 16, 1943, the food coupons listed below would be honored for the purchase of an ounce of cheese per person, and a half-pound box of laundry soap per family. It also announced the *Service du Travail Obligatoire* (STO), the Compulsory Work Service in Germany, for all French men age sixteen years and older. Whatever it was, it was bad news. Natalie carefully carried the candle to the dining room table so that she and Hélène could tackle their homework.

"Papa is in Switzerland now, where the best doctors work," Maman had said. It was good to know Papa had the best doctors. It meant he was coughing less, and when he no longer coughed, he would come home. In response, Natalie asked for Papa's address.

Maman replied, "What's the use? We can't write to Switzerland. Nobody can."

"Why not?"

"Switzerland is a neutral country. No one can get in or out. Only the Swiss can, or those willing to climb over very high mountains. There are guards with guns all along the borders."

That was awful. Still, Natalie waited impatiently for Papa, who would find a way to come back and make sure they were safe. She wondered whether she'd have the patience needed to wait until his return, when she could ask him about *Kristallnacht*, *sabotage* and *forgers*.

She had guessed what Gestapo meant because she heard the word every day, at school, on the streets, at the shops, even at the small Protestant church Maman insisted that she and Hélène attend on Sunday mornings. Mr. Gestapo was someone like a judge who could send anyone to prison, and decide who would be shot. She alternated between worrying about Maman and Papa. At present, it was easier to think about Papa.

Natalie knew she wasn't Papa's favorite, because Papa loved his three girls equally, but he was good to her. Once, when only Hélène was invited to a party, he had taken Natalie to a strange and beautiful place called a Mosque. Natalie had wanted to see it again with him before he became sick. She remembered Papa before he needed Swiss doctors, scooping his three girls up together in his arms, twirling around, calling them his little *Papagenas*, from a story about a magic flute. Doctors. Natalie liked thinking of doctors. They could not help Maman, but they would help Papa. Good doctors could do magical things.

Chapter 8

A Plucked Chicken

Maman was gone at least two hours, while the sirens howled, as they often did. When the all clear sounded, about 11:30 p.m., Maman still had not returned. Natalie sat in front of the grammar book she'd pulled out of her satchel hours ago, unable to concentrate on the exercises due in the morning. Each time she heard a faint sound, she thought it meant that Maman was reaching home.

She took the candle to the kitchen to wash the bowls, spoons and pan she'd used to make dinner. She had to use cold water, since the gas was out. She put away the dishes, and swept the kitchen before resuming her vigil, eyes smarting.

Ten minutes later, well after midnight, a woman with untidy hair piled high on top of her head walked in. Her lipstick was smeared. She spoke with Maman's voice, "You should be in bed! I look like a whore, I'm sure. Never mind. I brought home a chicken for tomorrow, I mean, later today, since it's almost one o'clock." Maman explained that she had gone to Papa's Swiss friends, the Remidoux, the only people who gave them good food from time to time since the Swiss bypassed most food restrictions.

"Imagine," Maman said, "Ginette was giving a birthday party for Edouard. She opened the front door, rushed me upstairs without a word, and spread lipstick on my mouth. She wrapped an Indian shawl around my shoulders. Downstairs, Edouard filled a glass and thrust it in my hand a minute before the Germans came in. I was transformed into one of their guests."

"Your bicycle?" Hélène asked, moving close to Maman.

Maman took off her coat. "Let me finish. The Germans lined us up. They only found a bunch of jolly neutral Swiss toasting their host. Believe me, I emptied my glass without hesitation. After everyone left, Edouard brought in my bicycle, which I'd dropped in the bushes around the corner. He oiled the chain, while Ginette wrapped up some cheese and this chicken for us."

Hélène craned her neck. "What a horrid chicken! It has no feathers."

Maman said, "Just as well. I won't have to pluck it."

For that whole week, they ate real dinners and went to bed without yearning for more. Maman saved the bones, gnawed clean by the children, to make broth from shriveled rutabagas, some white beans, an onion someone had left in the mailbox and dandelion greens growing wild the garden.

Chapter 9

The Tree-Trunk Man

Natalie proudly wrote 1943 on all her assignments because she would have her twelfth birthday in August. This was her last year of grade school with Madame Leverdier. Next year she would proudly go to the secondary school with Hélène.

For the third day in a row, the canteen lunch ladled into the children's tin plates consisted of smelly boiled cabbage with hard Lima beans. She forced herself to eat three spoonfuls. Then she dumped the rest into the plate of a girl who was always hungry and clamored for more.

Natalie scraped the bits left in her plate into the bucket behind the trestle table, and slipped her plate back into her cloth bag to wash at home, ready for the next day. Because she finished her lunch first, she was at the front of the line to lead out. Her friend, Rose, joined her at the door, making cat's cradles with odd bits of string.

Behind them, girls sang and argued, while the teacher admonished the slowpokes still sitting down. The canteen workers dragged slop buckets away. Through the din, Natalie heard dry claps followed by the screeches of a saw cutting hardwood. Before she could nudge Rose, a bellowing, helmeted German in a black uniform rushed up the steps, purple-faced with rage, eyes bulging, mouth stretched wide. He aimed his bayonet at Natalie, about to spear her through the tummy.

Rows of girls pushed her from behind. There was no room to retreat. In fear, Natalie's mouth filled with saliva, tasting of metal. Two more German soldiers ran up behind the first who made a sweeping gesture, clearly ordering the men to surround the building. Natalie's tummy became hard as wood. Voices hesitated and died. Madame Leverdier hurried through a crowd of children.

The helmeted German with the rifle shouted, "Two of your dirty Resistance men are hiding here, we know it. Common thieves, scum of the earth who steal food coupons from their countrymen. We'll shoot them—in front of you—as soon as I find them."

"There's no one here but schoolgirls and three canteen workers. Feel free to check," Madame Leverdier offered with arch courtesy. "Now I must take the children back to school."

"No school!" the German roared, his gleaming bayonet again aimed at Natalie's belly. "Curfew, until we find them. Don't worry," he added with a lopsided smile. "It won't take long. We always find your men."

Natalie pressed her tongue against the roof of her mouth and made fists to keep from being more afraid.

"Since they can't go back to school, the children need time to walk home."

"Five minutes, then we shoot on sight." The German officer clicked his heels before rushing through the startled crowd of girls into the kitchen.

Madame Leverdier stood, a hand on Rose's shoulder. "No more school today, *mes enfants*. Go straight home. If no one's home or you live too far, walk with a friend. You can go home later, when the curfew is lifted."

Wooden shoes clanked down the steps. Some girls held hands without speaking.

"Come with me," Rose whispered.

Rose lived on the other side of the school with her mother and her little brother, in a house under maple and flowering chestnut trees. Rose's father, an Englishman, had been in England on business when the Germans invaded France. He couldn't return home. They had no news of him.

Natalie and Rose ran together to the intersection. Rose crossed the street, but Natalie, feeling sick, slowed down. In the space in front of the town hall, lay a fallen tree trunk. Where did it come from? There were no trees on the main street. A German soldier stood above the fallen tree repeatedly stamping his black-booted leg down on it, as if to break it in two.

Natalie advanced. With a new wave of fear, she noticed a movement in the trunk. It was a man she'd mistaken for the tree, a man with his head turned toward her, lying like a dog run over by a car. The soldier jabbed and punctured pale coils he prodded upward from below the man's belt. Natalie's legs refused to move.

Leaflets with Lorraine crosses lay scattered about the fallen man. He moaned. Blood drooled out of his mouth. He opened his eyes and jerked. Knees buckling, Natalie saw that the pale, glistening coils the German threw in the air with his bayonet came out of the man's belly. His bowels. Her stomach was now a cage filled with boulders.

"*Venir, jeune fille, drôle*," "Come, young girl, funny!" The man in uniform laughed, beckoning in choppy French.

Forward, Natalie told her legs. Left foot down on the ground. Right foot off the ground then down. Left foot off the ground. Forward. Down. Right foot up. Down. Again. Again. Again. As she carried her cage, the boulders turned into biting rats. The cage was so full, it was bound to burst soon between her legs.

Because she hiccupped, she couldn't run. Rose had left her behind. Sirens shrieked. The grace period was up. The Germans were about to shoot. No shrub was large enough to hide her. Natalie staggered along, sweating and vomiting as she turned into a side street. Walk, walk, walk, further and further away. At last, she found herself in front of Rose's house. The ground swayed under her feet as she reached the gate. She stumbled into the garden. The rats inside her had multiplied. Helpless, Natalie squatted on the ivy under a tree for a long time. There was nothing inside her but foul, boiling water. She pushed her thumbs into her sides, then her fists, to lessen the spasms. Then, doubled over, shivering, she reached the front door.

"You didn't have to go to the bathroom in the garden!" Rose cried, opening the door. "Mummy, Natalie's here, but she looks...odd."

"Come in, my dear," Mrs. Gregory said from the door.

"I can't," Natalie whispered, shivering.

"You can't go home during curfew. It isn't safe. Won't you come in?"

Filled with shame, Natalie confessed she had soiled herself.

Madame Gregory expressed no disgust. She took Natalie's elbow. "There's nothing a bit of warm water won't clean. Come, come, there's a good girl."

In the bathroom, Madame Gregory washed Natalie as if she were a baby, with Rose looking on. "Lend her your striped socks and a pair of panties, Rosie, my love, and bring down the shawl and your slippers."

Partially dressed in Rose's clothes, Natalie sat limp in a wing chair while Madame Gregory went to make tea.

Returning, she handed Natalie a tea cup, "Drink your chamomile, it's good for you."

Natalie's teeth clattered against the cup.

"She's sweating, so she has a temperature," Rose said.

Madame Gregory said, "She'll be fine after a rest; won't you, *ma chérie*?"

Natalie sat wrapped in the pink shawl, knees up, feeling numb. She would have liked more shawls around her, but she couldn't find her voice to ask. Madame Gregory brought her a hot water bottle before calling Maman. Natalie marveled. Madame Gregory knew what to do without fuss or reproaches. Natalie whispered, "*Merci*, madame."

"No-no, you'd do the same for my Rose. Would you like to sleep a while?"

"Oh no!" Natalie protested. Anything might happen if she slept. She touched her tummy from time to time. "I'm fine now." To prove it, she took two sips of her chamomile and tried to smile at Rose's mother.

Rose read riddles to her out of the latest *Journal de Suzette*, a children's magazine. Madame Gregory was cutting a jacket out of one of her husband's winter coats for Rose, because she'd spent her textile coupons on fabric to make pants for Roger, Rosie's brother. The little boy played on the rug with tiny wooden zoo animals. Natalie kept still so as not to shatter the peace of the moment.

Rose said, "Why did you stop at the town hall? I ran across the street; I was too afraid of them."

Madame Gregory turned to Natalie. "Them?"

Words refused to come. Natalie pointed to her tummy.

"Your tummy hurts again?"

Natalie shook her head "no."

"Rosie thought she heard shots. That's not what you saw is it?"

"No," she managed to say. She raised her elbow. Pointing to her tummy, she pretended to poke out its contents with circular movements, keeping her eyes on Madame Gregory, imitating the jerking of the man on the ground, his eyes rolling back, his open mouth.

Madame Gregory was silent so long that even little Roger noticed. He waited, a toy zoo animal in each hand. Finally, she sighed. "We must have faith that very soon, things will improve. You'll see."

How could things get better? What could make the Germans weak? People had tried for years, yet things were still terrible.

Natalie was too numb to ask Rosie's mother what would happen if things didn't improve soon. She never wanted to go outside again. Here she had no pain. More Germans arrived all the time. Wave after wave till it felt as if there was no room left in France for French people. What will happen to me, to Rose, to all of us? Natalie wondered. If she asked, she would start crying so hard that she would not be able to stop.

When Natalie came home from the Gregorys' house, Maman asked no questions. Natalie wasn't surprised. Maman disliked talking about bodies. Maman sat at her black typewriter, a loan or gift from Madame Remidoux, her Swiss friend, an open book beside her. Her fingers dipped far down over mysterious keys. She spent much time practicing.

Natalie went to bed after a dinner of half a rutabaga and the white part of a leek. They shared a small red apple for dessert.

When Easter came with the usual school break, Maman told Lilla that the Easter rabbit couldn't come with his year with his chocolate eggs because of the war. When school started again after the two-week break, the desk next to Natalie's remained empty. Rose hadn't returned to school. Perhaps she had the flu. After a week, Rose was still absent.

Carrying her school bag and canteen after school, Natalie made a detour past her friend's house. No one answered when she rang the bell. Three days later, accompanied by Lilla, Natalie again walked by Rosie's house on the way home.

"Oh," was all Lilla said, a hand over her mouth.

At first, Natalie thought they'd taken the wrong turn. The trees that had spread wide fans of branches over the house were reduced to stumps. The house looked naked. Three cars, black and shiny, lined up on the street. A swastika flag undulated in front, hanging from Rosie's upstairs window. The blood-red fabric hung low, its ugly black-armed Nazi Party symbol dancing in a white circle as it waved above the doorway, casting shadows over the entry. Chauffeurs with black gloves and black uniforms joked with one another, leaning against the cars, lighting cigarettes.

"Rose!" Natalie wanted to shout. Rosie was gone, so were her mother and her little brother. Were they caught? Were they safe? Would she see them again? When? Natalie's heart thudded. She thought of telling Maman, who might comfort her, but knew Maman couldn't help. She had too many problems already. Besides, she'd rather practice typing, rapidly turning pages of her book, rather than answer questions; her fingers never ceased to click on the black keys.

Natalie closed her eyes. Rose hadn't had time to say goodbye, but right now Natalie imagined Rose was sending her a postcard, telling her when she would be back. Yes. The Gregorys had found a boat, just large enough for them, with a clever crew leaving that night at high tide for England.

Natalie saw shimmering waves of a retreating tide relentlessly pulling the little boat away from the coast of Normandy. Rosie's little brother slept on deck with a green and yellow toy parrot in each hand. Madame Gregory covered him with her pink shawl. Across the channel, Mr. Gregory waited, first in line on the dock, one hand like a visor over his eyes. In his other hand, he held a tricolor bouquet of balloons bobbing in the wind.

That evening, Natalie didn't want any dinner. In her room, she only took off her skirt and pullover. She put her two pairs of pajamas over her underwear. She made herself small under the covers. She had lost another treasure.

Chapter 10

Dark Journey

It must be a dream. Natalie turned over on her side in the good warmth of her bed. She heard an insistent voice as sheet and blankets were pulled away from her. Was it the German officer? No, it was Maman speaking urgently in a voice which frightened her. Natalie found herself shivering at the foot of the bed, slipping on her warmest clothes, clothes passed down from Hélène, who'd inherited them from a neighbor's niece. Maman handed her the hairbrush.

Natalie yawned, still sleepy but worried. "Where are we going?"

"Away with Tante Pauline, by train. Hurry, hurry up!" Maman carried a small suitcase downstairs.

"*Je n'ai pas fini mes devoirs.* I'm not done with my homework," Natalie mumbled as she stumbled downstairs in the dark.

Maman gave her a quick hug. Natalie wanted more hugs, longer ones.

"Forget about homework," Maman said—Maman, who always insisted on homework.

Natalie slipped on her jacket. In the right pocket, she fingered a couple of crumpled paper fish she'd kept for good luck. They were left over from April Fool's day, a few weeks ago.

It was only after she sat down in a black taxi moving

along unlit streets that Natalie realized that Maman had gone back into the house after locking the door, so now she sat alone next to Tante Pauline. Natalie felt her eyes water. Maman hated tears. Crying was for babies, she often said. But Natalie, forgetting she would be twelve years old in the summer, wept, and begged Tante Pauline to take her back home to ask Hélène to come along.

"How immature you are for a fifteen-year-old," Tante Pauline remarked.

"I'm not fifteen!" Natalie protested. "Hélène is fifteen. I'll be twelve in August."

"It doesn't matter how old anybody is," the dark shape of Tante Pauline said in a loud whisper, "because there is a war. Everyone must behave all the time." She added, "You might be able to see Papa, who is out of the sanatorium, resting in my house in Switzerland where there is no war."

Natalie was instantly calmed. Would she really see Papa? He must be doing well then. Papa had left so long ago that she couldn't remember the last time he'd kissed her. She knew what he looked like from a little photo Hélène had given her three years ago. Only his eyebrows seemed soft. The rest of him looked stiff as if he were only playing at being a Naval officer in a uniform with shiny buttons. She remembered him singing, hugging his girls in one giggling bunch, calling them "little *Papagenas*."

They rushed into a train station where locomotives spewed stinking black smoke. They had to fight their way into their car and found their seats saved by stern Oncle Marc. There were so many people that the door of their compartment could not close. Still more people came in. Natalie sat down and closed her eyes, wondering what a *Papagena* was, trying to hear Papa's voice in her head. He'd told her, but she'd forgotten.

Natalie sat next to Pauline, opposite Oncle Marc, who'd met them at the train station in Paris. The train was slow, full of sweaty people. Nobody spoke much. Papa's older brother looked only a little like him. Natalie wanted to forget Oncle Marc and Tante Pauline, but even with her eyes shut she saw the parting in Oncle Marc's dark hair plastered to his head and the grooves on the sides of his nose.

As for Tante Pauline, she was hard to ignore because she smelled of perfume. She never had wrinkles or stains on her clothes, and she did not give kisses. She was as tall as Oncle Marc, but she was flat and thin, with dull blue eyes. She shrugged when Natalie murmured, "Where is Hélène?" and "Is she with Maman and Lilla?" or "Where are we going?"

"Can't talk about this now. Later maybe," Pauline whispered and scowled to hush her.

The train stopped at every station and filled with even more people who stood in the aisles, leaning against other people. Some sat on suitcases in the passage. After some hours, Germans in gray-green uniforms with helmets and pistols boarded the train, poking their heads into each compartment several times. Natalie crossed her fingers for luck, pressing hard, keeping her hands in her pockets. Tante Pauline prepared papers to show the Germans when they returned to inspect their documents. The French inspector took their tickets from Oncle Marc and handed them back to Natalie with a tired smile. On the top ticket, she read, "April 26, seat number 6."

Twice they had to change trains. Pauline had brought a thermos filled with tea, and some cookies. People pushed others aside to grab seats. There was no lunch, no sandwiches, no restaurant car. In the evening, in the fog, the train reached a valley with a river in a village called *Abondance*. Oncle Marc carried his suitcase and Natalie's small one.

Tante Pauline held onto hers and Natalie's small rucksack as they entered the dark of a hotel with only six rooms. There were no pictures on the walls.

In the cold white room with a black cross over the dresser, Tante Pauline drilled Natalie. "On no account must you admit you're the daughter of a Jewish woman. If anyone asks, you must say that you're on your holiday with your parents. Understood?"

"Oui," Natalie said sulkily. Trying to change the conversation, she said, "I need my pullover."

"Don't just say, 'Oui.' That's impolite. Say, '*Oui*, Maman. Please may I have my pullover?'"

Intentionally, Natalie mispronounced "Maman." She didn't want to call Pauline Maman. "M'mon, can I have it?" was all she said.

They ate a bowl of soup at the hotel. A while after going to bed, through half-shut eyes, Natalie saw Oncle Marc hand Tante Pauline a booklet. Because she was Swiss, Tante Pauline could enter Switzerland by train without a problem any time she wanted. But Natalie had no papers.

"Here's your passport, Pauline. Take it. Do you realize," Oncle Marc grumbled, "that without the kid, we'd be in Montreux by now, instead of taking insane risks?" He sat on the empty bed. "Just because the girl looks like my brother doesn't mean she is our everlasting responsibility! When will she go home? Tell me that!"

Tante Pauline didn't answer.

With a pounding heart, Natalie wondered whether she'd be dumped somewhere in the dark. How could she walk alone along the railway tracks for a long, long time in the dark before getting home? What if a train came? She would hear it, of course, but where would she hide?

Oncle Marc said, "Maman wanted to take in sweet

Hélène, the little one went to some teacher friend's and the girl's mother is hiding in France. Why can't this one stay in France?"

"I told you. No one offered. I didn't want her either but I had no choice. I couldn't leave her alone in their empty house, could I? Neither could she live by herself in our Paris apartment with you at work all day at the Health Center. Besides, Francis is looking forward to seeing her. It'll be good for him," she said.

For a brief moment, Natalie was happy. Papa was expecting her! But then Oncle Marc said that Papa tricked people. That was a lie, she knew it for sure.

"I was against it from the start! My brother has always tricked people into doing what he wants. I agreed to house the family invalid for a short time because my parents begged us to take Francis for a few weeks. Now he's taking full advantage of us," he grumbled.

"I don't think that's quite fair," said Tante Pauline.

How could Papa be an invalid? Natalie asked herself. Invalids were crippled people. Papa had a bad cough, and he must be better or he could not leave the hospital.

"No, you wouldn't think it fair, but then you didn't grow up with him. He was the blue-eyed wonder, the charmer, with everyone at his feet. And it seems to me you happen to be his latest victim."

They lowered their voices. Natalie couldn't make sense of what she'd heard. Her fear intensified. Her middle fingers had covered her index fingers by themselves.

"Do you realize the danger, not to speak of the cost, of taking a child with you illegally? A Jew at that!"

"Shhh," Tante Pauline whispered, "she'll hear you."

"She's dead to the world."

Tante Pauline said, "How will you come to Lausanne

this time? Can you get another leave?"

"I already told them. I'll come as before. By train, since the Red Cross is looking once more for a volunteer doctor from Paris to accompany another convoy of sick children. I've applied. Shouldn't take long. I could be in Lausanne in two weeks. I'm covered for the work in Paris, but I need to see what they've been up to in the Montreux lab." Natalie heard him rub his dry hands.

"That is," he grumbled, "unless someone finds out about this insane business."

Natalie pictured Maman slipping out of her French hiding place, secretly climbing through a window at night to see Lilla, kissing her good night in the strange basement of a strange house, on a strange street. How did you find people when you didn't know the name of their street or their town? Where was Maman now? Did Maman hide well enough? She worried.

Natalie was cold all over. She dared not remind Oncle Marc or Tante Pauline that she had no passport or they would leave her behind. She was too far from Le Vésinet to find her way home. Worst of all, if she went back, she wouldn't see Papa. Without him, things could never go back to normal.

On their second day in the village of *Abondance*, the three of them took a long mountain ride up a twisting road in an old bus. They saw nothing except four cows in the distance, and a few dilapidated cabins in an immense meadow of foxgloves and bluebells. Below the road, a roaring stream boomed and disappeared inside dark woods. Later, they went for a picnic near the village hotel. Oncle Marc carried a picnic basket as they climbed to knoll near a copse of trees. They ate bread and cheese and a small hard apple in a patch of yellow daisies and weeds shedding wispy cotton on the grassy slope, pinkish against the pines. Oncle Marc only talked to Tante Pauline, who sat on a rock. Natalie blew on parachute seeds. Then they walked back, one behind the other, to the hotel.

Now that it was dark, Natalie found it hard to breathe. At a dinner of bread served with a piece of grey meat, Natalie ate only the bread because she could barely swallow.

"I want you to go to bed now," Tante Pauline said. "We will leave very early in the morning. We have a long walk ahead of us."

Natalie didn't brush her teeth before getting into the white bed without a comforter. She was worried, but she didn't protest because soon she'd see Papa. Instead, she curled into a ball, as afraid as she'd been at school when the furious German in black pointed his bayonet at her. She changed sides, knees pulled up, her hands in her armpits.

When Natalie woke up after hardly sleeping at all, Oncle Marc was saying goodbye to Tante Pauline. He didn't kiss her the way Papa used to kiss Maman. "Good bye," was all he said. He was going back to Paris.

Natalie brushed and braided her hair. She dressed in her plaid skirt and blouse.

Tante Pauline said, "Slip your blue blouse on top of the white one, and your dark skirt over the plaid one."

Natalie cried, "I can't. It won't button at the waist. It's too tight. "

"Use this safety pin, then wear your gray pullover over your red one," said Tante Pauline.

"It's tight under the arms." Natalie said, facing the blank windows where no shapes or stars shone. "I'm too warm."

Tante Pauline didn't listen. "You'll need to keep warm. We'll be walking a very long way. Keep it in mind."

It was still night when Natalie dragged her small suitcase out of the closet.

"What are you doing? Put that suitcase back where you found it."

"I must take care of it. The suitcase belongs to Maman, she will be angry if I don't bring it back home."

"Oncle Marc will pick it up later," Tante Pauline said.

When? He'd already left for Paris. But Natalie didn't dare argue with Tante Pauline because she wanted to see Papa. Maman would be angry when she found her suitcase missing. Suitcases were expensive. Everything was expensive. Natalie rehearsed in her mind how to explain it all to Maman.

With her small rucksack on her back, Tante Pauline set out with Natalie into the predawn mountain chill. There would be no breakfast. No trees were above their path as they went higher, though they could make out a tree line far below the patches of snow around them.

"Where are we going?" Natalie asked, feeling small and cold in the dark.

"To the baker's. He knows what to do. Be quiet." Tante Pauline turned up her jacket collar and kept pushing her index finger between the fingers of her gloves.

Natalie asked, "Why do your hands shake?"

"I'm cold."

Natalie didn't have gloves or a warm jacket. She was cold too, but proud not to be trembling.

When they arrived at the baker's, he motioned for them to hurry behind his shop and made them climb into his donkey cart. He drove them up and up a bumpy road to a farmer's who made them sit on the floor of his van behind bags of straw that shook dust on their faces. He spoke to them through the wooden partition, forbidding them to sneeze. "If someone hears you, the three of us will be shot then and there. I'm finished with this job. You're my last ones. Too risky, do you hear?"

Natalie pinched her nose to avoid sneezing. She breathed through her mouth and swallowed gritty bits that fell in. After many turns, the farmer spoke through the planks. "Hey! *Fichez le camp*. Scat before someone notices."

With the hiccupping engine running and the van barely stopping, Tante Pauline pushed and held the back door open. Natalie shoved straw bundles aside and jumped out. Tante Pauline jumped out after her, closing the back of the van with a peg on a string.

The cold air smelled clean. Tante Pauline picked straw off her skirt. Ahead was the trail partially hidden by low-growing plants. It was muddy. Their footsteps squished along as they passed a noisy spring bubbling into a carved log. After a half hour hike, they saw amid the patches of snow in the distance a dilapidated shed sitting on an outcrop of rocks.

When they reached it, Tante Pauline tried in vain to open the door. They stood without talking, waiting in the fog and wet grass for a signal. Tante Pauline paced by the shed, a hand shading her eyes, though it wasn't yet daylight. As her sandals and double pair of socks were saturated with dew, Natalie remembered the shoes and socks left in her suitcase at the hotel. "I have dry socks at the hotel," she murmured.

Tante Pauline's hand dropped. "You should have thought of that before we left the hotel."

Natalie's tears, warm, then icy cold, rolled down her cheeks. Tante Pauline didn't notice.

Sitting on a log, Natalie rocked herself in tiny motions. Hélène must be in Grand-Maman's home right now, drawing fancy dresses or lions and lizards on the pink wallpaper of her room, or working alone on her Latin. That would be better than standing in the fog on a mountaintop.

A cow lowed somewhere. The spring rushed below. What if someone saw them? The shed door opened like an explosion in Natalie's chest. A man came out. He spoke to Tante Pauline, pointing two hundred yards down to a tall fence lined with high rolls of barbed wire. The cold silk of darkness had thinned enough to reveal the silhouettes of five men with guns moving along the coils. The man brought a finger to his lips. "Italian guards. Nazis' good friends. They patrol the Franco-Swiss border along the river."

The guards stepped along the fence with a pack of dogs tugging at their metal leashes. As soon as they were gone the man said, "You have seven minutes before the five Italian guards come back. Follow the guide. Run!"

Her rucksack on her back, Tante Pauline, with a very cold Natalie on her heels, ran toward the fence where a slim man, almost a boy, silently beckoned them to follow. He crept along the barbed wire coils without a sound. At a dip in the rocks, where the barbed wire didn't quite meet the crumbling boulders, he vanished into a crevice.

It was almost daylight. The sky was pink. Behind Tante Pauline, who stumbled, Natalie, unfeeling from terror, squeezed into the depression. It was the tip of a stone funnel down which they advanced carefully to avoid dislodging rocks that would alert the guards. Tante Pauline was in such a rush that she never turned around to see whether Natalie was following.

Chapter 11

Crossing into Switzerland

Suddenly they were in the open, running away down the steep mountain. The slim boy had vanished. Natalie felt nothing except the trembling of her legs. Her hands were grazed from holding onto outcroppings of rocks. She longed to sit down. Didn't Tante Pauline say that once in Switzerland, they would be safe?

This time Tante Pauline took Natalie's hand, dragging her down toward another darkness. To avoid falling, they inched forward, crouching, holding onto tufts of low vegetation. There were shouts above them. Dogs barked, hideously close. The sky, suddenly exploded about them. All around them, bullets clanked against the rocky slope. Silver sparks flew about their feet and ankles, lighting bright blue gentians, the vivid starry blue flowers close to the ground.

Natalie flattened herself along the shadow side of rocks, her knees weak and heart beat so loud it surely could be heard over the whole valley. When all sound ceased, and the dust settled, she ran and staggered behind Tante Pauline past cottony edelweiss and fragrant short-stemmed vanilla orchids. There below them was a dazzling silver line—a Swiss river.

It was daylight, warmer. Mud dried on their clothes. Horseflies buzzed in a cloud above their heads. On they went, panting toward the foaming water at the edge of a forest.

Tante Pauline's voice was halting as she said. "Look for a bridge, to the left."

They looked, and as soon as they saw it, set off running until they collapsed on the moss. Tante Pauline removed her gloves. Beside her, Natalie knelt to scoop up the marvelous water in her cupped hands. Something tickled her ear. Hair brushed her face. She'd lost one of her ribbons because one of her braids had come undone. Though they were now in Switzerland, Natalie turned around to make sure no German officer holding her ribbon had seen her. They were barely across the border. German soldiers or the Italians with dogs on chains could still catch them since no one protected them.

Tante Pauline wiped her face with a lacy handkerchief and dropped her backpack to the ground. She joined her hands above her head and said in a funny voice, as if preaching from a pulpit, "Oh, God Almighty, Creator of the Universe, we thank you from the bottom of our hearts for leading us into Switzerland and leaving France with its endless problems behind. Only You know how much it cost me to undertake this trip with a mannerless child. We thank you for good weather, for the beauty of nature, for helping hands on our journey, for your protection and your many blessings."

As Tante Pauline enumerated God's blessings, starting with the sun that shone over them but omitting the merciless horseflies that bit them, Natalie retied her braids in front of her with her single ribbon and threw them over her head like a loop. She hoped that Tante Pauline's prayer would soon end, so they could move further away from the border, just a ten-minute climb from the river bank.

Tante Pauline kept talking to the sky for a boring long time. "Oh, Lord, make the child respectful and obedient! I confess she's not as I expected, being so immature." Then for no reason at all, Tante Pauline invoked Moses and Ezekiel. "Let's be grateful for the manna eaten in the desert. Amen," she concluded, pulling off her gloves. Surprisingly, she pulled her small handbag from the backpack and proceeded to powder her nose.

None of it had any bearing on escaping the Italian guards or crossing the border without a passport. All Natalie wanted was to reach the village and the mountain train that would take her to Papa. She couldn't wait to be safe again. She peeled off her gray pullover and her top skirt and waved them overhead to chase away the blue flies that drew blood from her cheeks, arms and legs. She knelt down to stuff her spare skirt into Pauline's backpack, without permission. Tante Pauline finally said, "Let's sit on the grass and have our snack."

They munched on cookies and withered yellow raisins. Three raisins fell around Tante Pauline's feet as she poured from the pouch into Natalie's hand. Natalie dove down, picked them up and stuffed them into her mouth.

"Those raisins are dirty. They needed rinsing. Is that how you were raised?"

"No," Natalie answered, "but we don't waste anything. Maman says wasting food is a sin."

Tante Pauline sighed. "The next stage," she said, "is to walk down to the village. It's a two-hour walk with you in tow. From there, we'll ride first in the mountain trolley and in a train after that."

Natalie wanted to say that it wasn't her fault that the village was two hours away. But it would do no good to argue with Tante Pauline who spoke more to the sky and to God than to her. She thought about the mountain trolley.

Along the bank, two unsteady tree trunks lay across the river, licked by spray erupting between jumbled rocks. That would have to do for a bridge. Arms extended for balance, Natalie and Tante Pauline progressed unsteadily along the moss-covered bark half sunk in the jumping water. On the other side of the river, way below, were six or seven structures as small as dollhouses. A Swiss village.

"For a while I didn't think we'd make it." Pauline sighed, sitting again on the grass, putting her gloves back on after replacing some hairpins.

Natalie was glad to be out of France. She didn't have to call Tante Pauline 'Maman' any longer and soon she would see Papa. "Is Switzerland a big country?" she asked.

"No," Tante Pauline said. "We are a very small country in the middle of Europe. The Germans could come any time they wanted, they are so close." Since Switzerland was small, it wouldn't take them long to find her. Perhaps because she was near her own home, Tante Pauline smiled for the first time, walking faster, thumbs hooked under the straps of her rucksack. Natalie followed, head down.

In the village, they drank water again, from a public fountain this time. Natalie was hungry, but she said nothing because if they took the time to buy a sandwich to share, they might miss the trolley that would take them down into the valley to board the train.

Once aboard the train, Natalie saw a Switzerland full of flowers. In a week, it would be May. Red and white geraniums bloomed around poles set in the middle of fountains in each neat village. Pink and purple cosmos swayed in gardens.

They stepped off the train at Montreux. Tante Pauline sat Natalie down on a bench in the waiting room of the station. "Promise me never, ever to touch your Papa. If you do, you'll start to cough, and you will have to go to the hospital."

"To die?" Natalie asked, incredulous. It didn't seem possible to die from coughing. She looked at Tante Pauline's hands with their many rings.

"Many people die in the hospital," Tante Pauline said, looking grave. "If you want me to take you to see your Papa, you must promise."

"I promise," Natalie muttered, feeling shattered. She had imagined hugging Papa so many times, and it would not be possible.

"Are you sure you understand?" Tante Pauline raised an index finger, like a teacher. Natalie nodded. Tante Pauline made a telephone call from a cabin in the station and then they sat in the very clean waiting room of the station.

Opening the compact she had saved in her pocket, Tante Pauline again powdered her nose. After a while, Pierre, Tante Pauline's gray-haired gardener-chauffeur arrived with Pauline's car.

"Welcome, Madame. Everything is ready. You'll be home in twenty minutes," Pierre said, speaking to Pauline but looking at Natalie with a smile. He took the rucksack from Pauline, opened the car door for her, waited till Pauline settled in the front passenger seat, and shut the door for her. He dropped her backpack into the trunk and let Natalie in the back.

At first, Natalie enjoyed having the back of the car to herself. She had plenty of room. She wished Hélène were with her, sitting on the folding side-stool opposite hers. They would kick each other's feet. She felt lonely. "Where is Hélène now, Tante Pauline?" she asked, hoping to hear some details.

Tante Pauline replied, "Probably with Grand-Papa and Grand-Maman."

"Is Lilla with her?"

There was no answer.

And Maman, where was she? Papa would know.

Chapter 12

Montreux

From the front, Tante Pauline's house looked like a sand-colored chateau without a moat. The trees on either side of the central alley had special shapes, like triangles or apples cut out of magazines. There were no dead leaves anywhere, no dead flowers, no brown petals on the rose bushes full of blossoms.

Pierre hurried ahead of Tante Pauline to the trunk of the car. He opened the car door for Tante Pauline, handing her the backpack. A fat maid with a lace-trimmed apron ran out to welcome Pauline. Natalie stood by.

"Say 'how-do-you-do' to Edith," Tante Pauline said.

Natalie extended a hand, which Edith didn't take. Instead she said, "Bonjour Mademoiselle." The three of them stood in the hall. Edith kept saying, "*Oui,* Madame, *oui,* Madame," while Tante Pauline gave her orders.

Glancing into the sitting room, Natalie saw silver candleholders on a table with photos. In a wood niche was a painting of a man in a hooded coat who looked at four birds on his hands. Below the painting she read the title, *San Francisco di Assisi.* He looked kind. She smiled at him.

There were flowers and cushions and pretty things everywhere. There was an ivory letter opener like Maman's, carved at one end, and flowers in two green glass vases.

Everything looked new. Edith took her to the kitchen and gave her a thick white drink. It was very good.

"Do you always drink cream in Switzerland?" Natalie asked.

"That was milk," Edith laughed. "This is cream, see?" Edith showed her a pitcher filled with something yellow. In Switzerland, then, milk wasn't pale blue. Natalie wished she could run out and tell Hélène, who had said their milk was blue because it was diluted with water. There was bread in an open bin on the counter. She didn't dare ask for a slice, though her stomach growled. She hoped they would soon eat dinner.

Edith showed Natalie her room, a pink and white one, with white furniture, and ran a bath for her in a bathroom with little soaps shaped like seashells. Edith let Natalie wash herself, but insisted on rinsing Natalie with a large sponge, even though she was old enough to do this alone. Then Edith brought an enormous fluffy towel to wrap Natalie in. Natalie sat on the edge of the tub while Edith brushed her hair. "My clothes, Edith, where are they?" she asked.

"In the laundry. Try those on."

On the bed sat four little piles. One was a stack of ironed short-sleeved blouses, one blue checkered, one white, and one pale green. Another pile was shorts, all navy blue. One pile was made of six pairs of new underpants, with labels still attached. There were also white cotton socks, rolled up in pairs. Two ironed dresses were draped on a chair by the table.

"These aren't mine," Natalie remarked.

"They're yours now. From the Red Cross," Edith said, adding, "I hope you don't mind."

"I like new clothes," Natalie admitted, "but I don't get many, because I have to wear Hélène's clothes when they get too small for her. Hélène, that's my big sister." A lump rose in her chest when she pronounced Hélène's name. "Can I wear that yellow dress with the tiny flowers to see Papa, just this once? I'll be careful not to wrinkle it."

Edith nodded. "I told you. All this is yours."

"You mean, to keep?" Maman would have saved the dresses for Hélène to wear on special occasions. "What if it doesn't fit?" she asked. Edith would take it away, of course.

"Then I'll adjust it."

Edith was nice. Natalie wriggled into the yellow dress, which fit around her body, though the full skirt was too long. She wished she could keep it on and rush downstairs to Papa.

"I'll make a quick hem. Would you like that? I have a needle and thread right here in this little box. See? It'll do for tonight," Edith said.

"You don't have a sewing machine? Maman has one, a Singer," Natalie said, twisting with impatience. She sat on the bed between the shorts and the socks, in her underpants, watching Edith who turned the dress inside out and made large stitches before cutting the thread with her teeth when she was finished.

The dress was right side up again. Natalie stood, arms raised. Edith slipped it over her head, gave it a few tugs and tied the belt behind her back.

She was ready for Papa.

Chapter 13

Reunion with Papa

Tante Pauline led her to the second floor then through two sets of doors. Natalie expected to see Papa in the navy uniform he wore in her little photograph. Instead, in a narrow bed with pillows behind him, lay a thin man in a white shirt and plaid tie. Natalie leaned toward the pale man. She looked at him, remembering the Christmas carol Papa used to whistle. If he sang about angels in the countryside, she would know this man in bed was her father. In a dress with frilly sleeves and a pattern of tulips, Tante Pauline was all smiles. She grabbed Natalie by the elbow. "You promised," she whispered into Natalie's ear. "Remember you get very sick."

Natalie heard Papa's voice when the man spoke her name and opened his arms. "Natalie, my *Papagena,* Natalie."

"Francis, *mon cher* Francis, here we are!" said Pauline. As she quickly took a step forward, her grip loosened enough for Natalie to dash ahead and throw herself at Papa, hugging him at the waist.

"It's so good to see you," Papa said, passing his hand over her hair, resting it on her shoulder.

"Maman has to hide, Papa. Can she join us?"

"Edith is waiting to wash your hair before dinner, Natalie," Tante Pauline interrupted. "We just wanted you to know we'd arrived safely, Francis. We'll be back later."

"Did you have to disappoint me so soon? I told you never

to touch him!" Tante Pauline grumbled outside Papa's room.

Natalie didn't care. She had seen Papa! He'd spoken to her! She would see him many, many times since they were in the same house. Bursting with happiness, Natalie ran away from her to take off her own flowered dress. She hurried to slip on a pair of shorts and the white blouse so Edith could give her a shampoo. Then she went downstairs for her first dinner in Montreux.

From now on, everything would be better. She had Papa. All she needed was to figure out how to get him to France.

Edith had washed her hair, careful not to let soapy water make her eyes burn. It was almost dry when Natalie stepped into the dining room for the first time. Only Edith was there, folding napkins into flower shapes at each place.

"Where are the bread bags, Edith?" she asked, so she'd know where to sit.

"Bread bags? Whatever for? The bread goes into the breadbasket, of course."

"You don't slice the loaf and give us our slice for the day?"

"That slice would be stale! There is plenty of bread. Raisin bread for breakfast, two or three milk rolls per person for lunch and dinner when guests come, and sliced breads at dinnertime."

Natalie's mouth watered. When Edith had her back turned, Natalie snatched a slice of white bread from the sideboard and slipped it in her pocket, muttering something about wanting a handkerchief. In her room, she stuffed the whole slice into her mouth. She saw her bulging cheeks in the bedroom mirror and chewed happily on the delicious bread. She wiped her mouth, brushed off crumbs from her top and ran back down.

Edith was arranging fruit in a glass and silver basket. "Pierre goes to the bakery at six every morning," she explained, as if Natalie had not run upstairs, "I tell him how much to buy."

"It's that easy?"

Edith looked at her strangely before nodding slowly. "Yes, it's that easy."

Dinner was quiet. Tante Pauline had invited an old friend of hers, who came in high heels with lots of make-up on her face and neck, carrying a satchel full of fabric samples so Tante Pauline could choose among them before going to her dressmaker. The two women barely spoke to Natalie, who let a dinner roll fall onto her lap, hiding it under her napkin. When the ladies raised their glasses to wish each other good health, Natalie pushed the roll from under her napkin into the pocket of her shorts. Then she started on the veal in cream sauce Edith had served with fresh peas and new potatoes. If Papa was hungry, she could bring him rolls.

Tante Pauline said, "The child is falling asleep at the table. Go to bed, Natalie."

Natalie said a low, "Thank you." Then she climbed the stairs to her room on the third floor. She took out her bread roll. It was flatter but still soft. She only ate half for pleasure, because she'd eaten a good dinner. She pushed the rest of the roll under her pillow.

The following evening, a man who worked at Oncle Marc's lab in town came to dinner with his wife. Tante Pauline wore a pale blue dotted pink dress and a gold pin in the shape of a smooth leaf with three pearls in the middle, like drops of water. Maman, too, had pearls, but as earrings. The three adults talked together, sometimes in German, so Natalie didn't understand.

Natalie took the new bread roll from her napkin, munch-ed, and helped herself to another when Edith passed the basket around. Since the adults ignored her, she had time to eat her meal, get second helpings of rice and grilled tomatoes topped with melted cheese, and enjoy the apple juice in her wine glass, instead of drinking water. It was a great feeling to be so full.

Tante Pauline had noticed her after all. "Before you leave the table, you must excuse yourself and say, 'Thank you, Tante Pauline.' When your uncle is with us, you will thank him too." She shook her head with a sigh and began speaking German.

Natalie guessed Tante Pauline was complaining to the couple about her niece's lack of manners. She clenched her jaw with irritation. With the grown-ups on their way to the sitting room, she started to clear the plates.

Tante Pauline turned around. "What are you doing? Leave that alone. That's Edith's job."

Instead of talking with Papa, Natalie had to sit with the grown-ups in the sitting room with nothing to do. After some boring minutes, she stood up and asked, "May I be excused?"

Tante Pauline nodded.

Natalie muttered, "Merci, Tante Pauline." There was no hugging or kissing, no wishes of "sweet dreams," "sleep well" or even "good night." She must repeat her thanks every night, to be dismissed without smiles, she guessed.

She touched the lump the roll made in her pocket. She could get rolls for Papa. She would ask him tomorrow. She pretended that Hélene was also getting ready for bed in her room. It was the perfect time to softly tell her all about the dinner, and how Pauline was mean.

Chapter 14

A Good Luck Stone

Natalie missed breakfast her next day at Tante Pauline's because she slept thirteen hours. Edith woke her up at 10 a.m. She only had time to swallow a glass of Ovaltine in the kitchen before she had to go to town with Edith, who'd been instructed to buy her a swimsuit. Once there, Natalie dawdled on the street, examining the well-dressed people. Natalie wanted to remember everything to tell Papa what she had seen. She thought about him constantly.

Back at Tante Pauline's for lunch, there was toasted, buttered white and brown bread cut into triangles with mushroom soup, a quiche with plenty of ham, a tomato salad, cheese and chocolate mousse with two kinds of cookies. It was unexpected, unbelievably good, and there was so much that Natalie ate seconds of everything.

It was a sunny and warm day, so after lunch, Tante Pauline phoned her friend. They took Natalie in the car with them to the lake. Once there, it was as if she were only another bag of towels. The women lay side by side on rented deck chairs, each with a towel under their head, spreading lotion on themselves, their eyes hidden behind sunglasses, chatting. Natalie, in her new striped swimsuit with green dots, sat on the pebbly beach, listening to the clanging of varnished rowboats in shallow water and the talk of some fat little boys. If Hélène had come, they would have fun. She quietly started to build a tower of flat stones behind the two women's chairs to eavesdrop.

"Did I tell you about that aunt of hers? I had spoken to her, waiting in line at the baker's. They nabbed her as she stood behind me, a minute after three in the afternoon."

"What's special about 3 p.m.?" the friend asked.

"They must do their shopping between one and three when the shops are closed, you see."

"Didn't you tell her?"

Tante Pauline raised a shoulder. "What use would it have been? There was nothing she could have done."

Somebody's aunt had been arrested. One of Maman's sisters? Natalie wanted to know. Yet at the same time, she didn't, because she'd have to tell Papa and she must not bring him bad news. It would give him nightmares. She plugged her ears with her fingers and walked along the pebbly beach.

She stepped into the lake up to her knees, though the water was quite cold, keeping her arms above the splashing blue water, glancing at beautiful clothes careless people left on the rocky beach when they swam. Maman could have made good clothes out of them! She tread water, looking for stones, till she found a lovely blue one. A good luck stone for Papa.

Chapter 15

Pierre

Natalie spent time in her room because Tante Pauline had given her a stack of paper and colored pencils. She tried to draw the beach with the rows of colored umbrellas. The water was the hardest to do, even when she tried to copy how it was done in magazines and picture books. What she really wanted was to run into Papa's room. Sadly, that was not allowed. Still, her legs wanted to run. Dropping her papers and pencils, she wandered outside.

Soon she found herself in the back garden where Pierre was kneeling in his dungarees beside freshly dug soil. She stood in silence next to him.

"Can I help?" she finally asked.

"You can help plant the poppies. See, all you need to do is drop a pinch of seeds from this packet into the holes I'll make." He didn't wear gloves. He pushed two fingers into the brown soil, making a funnel hole.

"Like this?" Natalie took pinches of black seeds and dropped them in. Pierre tapped soil into the holes when she was done.

"You want more work? Here." He pointed to the watering can. She half-filled it at the tap on the wall. That was all she could carry. The nozzle let out a spray like the spray bottle she used at home to moisten the laundry before ironing.

"I want something else to do." She needed to keep busy

because she had to wait such a long time before going in to see Papa.

"Why don't you ask Edith? You might get your new clothes dirty in the garden."

"It doesn't matter. They aren't new. Someone didn't want them, so the Red Cross gave them away. Edith said so."

"Someone will have to wash them, though, if you mess them up."

Natalie hadn't thought of that. "I'll go ask Edith. I still want to help."

Edith let Natalie shell peas and laughed when she ate raw ones as if they were candy. Later, Edith trusted her to set the silverware at each place for dinner as instructed. Natalie put three forks to the left of each plate, and three matching knives to the right, in order of size. The spoons and knives lay together like husbands and wives, but the forks were alone on their side. Natalie set them on the tablecloth as told, and made a face. The flatware arrangement was wrong, she decided. The spoon was like Maman. It had rounded sides. The spoons should lie by themselves.

Natalie picked up the forks and laid them alongside the pointy, serrated knives on the right side of each plate, thinking of thin Oncle Marc and narrow Tante Pauline. They belonged together. She set the dessert forks and spoons at the top of the each plate, all in the same direction on the damask cloth. This reminded her of the horses and greyhounds at the racetrack she'd seen many times from the train when Maman used to take her, Hélène and Lilla to visit Grand-Papa and Grand-Maman in Versailles before the Star of David rule. Satisfied, Natalie went to the kitchen. "Now I'll set the glasses," she told Edith.

"No," Edith responded, "I'll take care of the crystal glasses."

Edith was flustered because she was preparing a cheese soufflé. She might not notice that the knives and forks had changed places. And if she did, she might not have time to put them back.

For lunch, Edith always set two glasses at each place. For dinner, three, sometimes four glasses per person when guests came. Natalie only had two, one for water and one for juice. She felt it was unfair not to let her set glasses on the table, because at home, she set the entire table by herself with glasses and everything else for the whole family. Natalie sat in silence at dinner. From under her eyelashes, she watched Oncle Marc and Tante Pauline absentmindedly returning their forks to their usual places, talking about someone called Blum. No one commented on the silverware. Once in her room, Natalie told Hélène about Pierre and planting poppies. And how could Papa be an invalid? Invalids were crippled people. Papa had a bad cough, but she thought he must be better or he could not have left the hospital.

Chapter 16

Queen Anne's Lace

As a surprise, Tante Pauline gave Natalie a book called *Heidi.* Natalie loved it because the girl lived with her kind grand-pere in the Swiss mountains. Heidi managed to make her paralyzed friend walk again. Natalie must think of a way to make Papa healthy again. If she thought about it hard enough a good idea would come, and they could go home together. Perhaps she had misjudged Tante Pauline, who had given Natalie her own volume of *Heidi.*

Natalie would have liked climbing a ladder to reach her bed, as Heidi must. But how horrid for Heidi who sleeps in a barn loft, on a mattress of prickly straw above smelly, moaning animals! It made her itch to think about it. She read and reread the Heidi story so often that soon she knew whole passages by heart. In that story, in the end, everybody was happy. The book was so good she did not even need to talk to Hélène in her head.

She also read children's books that Tante Pauline sometimes brought home from the library. Between books, Natalie swept the back porch, polished leather shoes, and spread white paste over her sandals, thinking only of Papa and why she couldn't stay in his room all the time. One day when she was feeling very sad, she wandered outdoors. Pierre asked, "Is anything the matter? You look forlorn, *petite demoiselle.*"

"I have nothing to do. Can I water the garden?"

"I just finished watering. But you could come with me to buy honeycombs from Mr. Nicolet, who is the beekeeper."

Pierre asked permission to take Natalie along and Tante Pauline agreed. Natalie sat proudly in the front of the truck next to Pierre. When they arrived, Mr. Nicolet brought his strange hat to show Natalie. "Look, Natalie," he said. "This is the helmet I wear on my head and shoulders so the bees don't sting me. Want to try it? You'd be safe inside." Natalie pushed it away, shaking her head, which made Mr. Nicolet and Pierre laugh. It was too much like a gas mask. If she wore it, she would not be able to breathe and she would die.

One Sunday, Natalie found herself alone in the garden because Pierre didn't work on Sundays. She took a walk outside the property. On each side of the road, where the grass and weeds had not been mowed, a profusion of Queen Anne's lace bordered the sidewalks. She would make a bouquet for Tante Pauline.

There, she knew she had a good idea. Maman enjoyed the wildflowers she and Hélène brought her, even those from Lilla who always cut the stems too short. Natalie picked as many as she could hold in one hand, pressing them against her chest when her hands were full, keeping the largest parasol bloom in the center of her bouquet. Just beyond the corner of the property, past green blackberries on a thorny bush, pinkish-purple flowers like sweet peas climbed the fence. Pierre called them vetch. She picked five lovely purple flowered stems and mixed them into the airy blooms. Maman would have loved it.

She retraced her steps to find herself face to face with Tante Pauline, who emerged from the back garden wearing a wide-brimmed hat, a book in one hand and three pale roses in the other.

"For you," Natalie said, happy to have something to offer. "They're pretty, the white ones with the purple dot in the middle," she went on, when Tante Pauline didn't take them.

Tante Pauline moved her well-manicured hand back and forth at knee level as if shooing away a cat. "Don't bring those indoors," she said, as if Natalie hadn't spoken. "They're full of bugs." Then she strode into the hallway, leaving Natalie alone.

Natalie stood with her face burning. "Tante Pauline is flat and thin, like a towel from the bottom of the pile. I hate Oncle Marc. He's so thin he's ugly, with his flat face. They're a knife and fork. I will call them the *Maigrichons*, the Skinnies," she told an invisible Hélène who clapped in appreciation of the waterless baptisms. "The Skinnies are very mean. She's Gricha, Skinna and he's Skinno. I won't call them Oncle and Tante anymore," whispered Natalie.

She trotted to the back of the house and up onto the terrace where a large folding umbrella advertising Evian water shaded a round metal table. Two smooth, shiny rocks and a canning jar full of water sat on the table to prevent the wind from dragging the checkered tablecloth away.

Natalie placed her bouquet on one of the canvas chairs, grabbed the jar, poured half the water out over the edge of the terrace, and sat on the floor with it to arrange her flowers inside. Then she got up, wiped her hands on her shorts and, holding the jar full of white and purple blooms with both hands, she placed it on the shaded table between the two grey rocks.

She stood back, her hands on her hips, to tell Hélène in her mind, "Skinna the witch, doesn't want my flowers inside her house, so I'll never bring her any again, but she didn't say I couldn't keep them outside. See? I don't care if she doesn't like them, because we do."

That was on Sunday. On Monday when she wandered out by the back door, she found her bouquet missing, but the glass jar, filled with water, stood on the table again.

She looked for Pierre, who let her do some watering. "I've done most of it," he said, "but you can water the chives and the parsley, over there, and give only a cup or two to the geraniums, no more. They don't like to be wet."

After lunch, Natalie found Edith sitting in the kitchen, knitting long beige and brown tubes curling like boas on her lap, their unfinished heads hanging from the needles.

"What are those?" Natalie asked.

"Sleeves for the pullovers."

Natalie peered at the knitting.

"Every time I start knitting, you stare at me. Why is that?" Edith asked.

"Because I don't know how to do it," Natalie admitted, feeling herself blush. Natalie would have loved to make a soft, warm scarf for Papa when he rested on his chaise longue on the balcony. Maman would like her to know.

"I can show you. It's not that hard. I'll get needles for you tomorrow."

When the thick wood needles came, Edith gave her lessons. Natalie was excited. She promised herself to work hard at it, but her fingers couldn't move fast like Edith's, and she couldn't make the regular clicking sounds Edith made with the needle tips. Also, the yarn was not soft and spongy as the ball of blue wool itself. On her fingers, it felt scratchy, and it was hard to remember how to wind it around to cast a single stitch. Edith spoke of tension. Tension meant the stitches must be the same size, not tight and not loose, to slide on and off the needle.

"Once you get the hang of it, you'll find yourself able to knit without looking at your work," Edith declared.

That was as hard for Natalie to believe as to believe in

God, although Edith had spoken without looking at her twin boas.

"Is this wrong? It's too tight," Natalie complained.

Edith put aside her knitting and examined Natalie's practice square. "No wonder. Why did you knit two stitches together here, and here? You're missing two stitches on that row, see."

It sounded as if Natalie had deliberately made mistakes or had caused the stitches to be missing, like chocolates from a row in a box. She stood, head down and humiliated, next to a seated Edith who unraveled her work. "There's a hole there because you made up a stitch on the third row. It'll be all right. Knit only the stitches on the needles, as I told you. Nothing in between."

Edith had pulled more wool away from the little square. Great curly loops of blue wool, waiting to be knit up again, lay on the impeccably clean kitchen floor. Though Edith spoke kindly, it was hard for Natalie to see her destroy some of her work.

"You're learning. We all have to start somewhere. It's slow at first. You're showing progress," Edith kept saying. But progress was very, very slow.

Chapter 17

Visiting Papa

The most important part of Natalie's day was going to visit Papa. In the morning, she trembled with impatience. She was allowed in as soon as Pierre had finished shaving him. The second most important part was waiting to see him. While she waited, Natalie sat facing the grandfather clock in the sitting room, by the photo table with the silver candlesticks. She tried to knit, or draw ducks or trace hazelnut or lime leaves in her scrapbook, until it was time to go in.

Tante Pauline went in to see Papa any time she wanted, as if Papa belonged to her, Natalie thought resentfully. She was allowed in to see Papa only twice a day, as she had done when he was at home, only then she could stay a bit longer. It was unfair. Natalie only went in at nine thirty in the morning and three thirty in the afternoon. When three thirty finally came, she often found Papa sketching. Sometimes he drew French sailors with pompoms on their hats, winding ropes or straining back to haul a net still in bubbly water. Once he drew a feather with such a gleam in the middle and fuzziness at the edges that Natalie, thinking it had fallen on the paper, tried to pick it up.

Papa beamed. "This is by far the best compliment I've ever received, *Petites Nattes*. I have something for you. Look behind you," he added.

She turned around and discovered a green, glazed pot with lily of the valley in bloom, set in a cardboard box. "It's the first of May today. French King Charles IX received some *Muguet,* lily of the valley, on the first of May a long time ago. He found it so delightful that each May first, he gave lily of the valley to the ladies of his court." He stopped to cough, a hand on his forehead.

"Other people copied him. It became a tradition, so that now, after more than four hundred years, we still do it! A lovely way for a king to say thank you to his ladies, don't you think?"

"Is it for me? To take to my room?"

Papa nodded. To him, Natalie gladly said, "Thank you."

Natalie inhaled the lemony fragrance from the white curly bells rising over long, smooth leaves.

Papa knew everything. He made everything interesting. He showed her his book of Alpine flora, his book of rare American birds, with witch-head bald eagles and tiny *oiseaux-mouches*, hummingbirds, with purple or golden-green throats and needle beaks, who weighed less than a flower. He let her handle a book of Greek sculptures and a dictionary, into which he placed blossoms to dry. Natalie put her fingers over the red tabs that separated the sections of his dictionary, one for each letter of the alphabet.

Papa asked, "How was your trip here with Tante Pauline?"

Perhaps Skinna hadn't told him. It had been frightening, but he wanted to know. So Natalie focused on the best parts and made sure she left out no details. Looking at the floor, she even confessed that she'd been terrified at times.

Papa looked at her sadly, saying nothing at first, staying very still in his bed. Then he said,

"Now you don't need to worry anymore. You are safe

here, and I love having you close." Then, slowly, he started to draw what she described seeing on the trip. He drew the mountain, the river, the meadows, a few bright blue gentians, the shiny train with varnished wood slats, fountains, and even cows with heavy bells. They made a game of it, calling it The Map Game.

"To travel, you must start where you are, *Petites Nattes*, at one edge of the map. You need to make a list of items to take on your journey and any obstacles there might be."

"Obstacles?" she asked.

"There could be red ants or bears or storms in the area."

"What do we do when there are obstacles?"

"We stay away from animals. We wear good shoes or boots to climb over the rocks." He stopped to catch his breath. "And we take raincoats, always, just in case." Papa had to breathe often in the middle of sentences, but he kept drawing until he grew tired and had to rest.

"Preparing for a trip, what is it called?" Natalie asked.

"It's called making a plan. That way you can safely go where you want to be."

Natalie thought of her trip with Tante Pauline. How much better it would have been if Tante Pauline had let her make a plan. Papa would have done so, of course. Papa thought of everything. Always.

Chapter 18

The Only Jew in Switzerland

One afternoon in May, Skinno—Natalie didn't want to use his new name to his face—came back for two weeks. Papa liked him, probably because Skinno was his brother. Natalie didn't. She disliked his wife Skinna less. Skinno strode into the sitting room where Natalie, sitting on a stool, was reading *Heidi*. She looked up at him and picked up a roll of her drawings, which she'd tucked under the stool.

"Oncle Marc, when you go back to France, will you take my drawings to Maman?"

"Fine." Skinno picked up the roll of drawings and plunked it on the piano as he sat on the bench. "Write a letter to Grand-Maman. She'll like that," he said as he played scales.

"I can't. Grand-Maman is mean to Maman, so we don't speak. Writing is like speaking, *n'est ce pas*?" Natalie said.

Skinno frowned. His mouth became a thin line. Natalie thought she'd better leave him alone. She went to her room to write Hélène a letter. She often spoke to Hélène in her head, but a letter was probably better. She hoped Papa could include it with one of his letters to Maman.

The next afternoon, Natalie burst into Papa's room. "Papa, I'm the only one."

"Really? Is that good?"

"I'm not sure."

Art books lay scattered on his bed with colored markers sticking out. "You mean, the only child here?" he asked.

"No, not that." Natalie untied and retied her sandals.

"Tell me," Papa said from his bed.

"I made a plan to see if I'm the only one. I looked in the shops and on all the streets and in the tramcars. People don't have stars on their coats here. So that means I'm the only Jew here," Natalie announced breathlessly.

Papa was grave. "In Switzerland, no one is forced to wear a star. Switzerland isn't an occupied country. We are free."

That was when Edith knocked. She brought in a glass jug filled with pear juice for Papa.

Natalie ran to her room for her colored pencils. She sat on her bed to think about what Papa had told her. Free? There were no Germans around, true, but she didn't feel free. She wondered whether Papa liked living in Switzerland or whether he must stay because he was sick. It would be rude to ask. She liked Switzerland, definitely. Switzerland was brimful of flowers. She never went to bed hungry. People smiled. The mountains were lovely and bluish. People had dogs and cats. She met two girls visiting their grandmother, and she played with them sometimes. She hated the Skinnies, of course. But she wanted to stay in Switzerland because it was so beautiful and, most important of all, Papa was there.

Chapter 19

A Glutton

After another trip in June, Skinno came back to Montreux. The town facing Lake Geneva was full of frilly, perfumed irises, many types of tulips, and rhododendron bushes covered in pink and purple blossoms. Natalie admired all the flowers as she and Skinna walked along the promenade, passing time, since they were too early to meet Skinno's train. He came for two weeks at a time. Natalie wished he would not come back. There were many large buildings and hotels from *La Belle Époque* along the lakefront, Skinna said. Everything in town looked freshly painted, impeccable, and new. Natalie was thrilled.

The next morning, Skinno caught up with Natalie on the upstairs landing as she was on her way to the garden.

"What is this?" He brandished what was left of the bread roll Natalie had saved under her pillow the night before. The others disappeared each day. Natalie guessed Edith threw the stale one out. "A thief in our midst! What do you have to say for yourself? Don't you dare claim that Edith put that in your bed!"

"I took—I took it," she stammered, "for tomorrow."

"Is that so?" His circumflex eyebrows rose. "What is to happen tomorrow?"

Natalie felt the floor tilt under her feet. It was too hard to explain that she was afraid there'd be no bread for breakfast. Her voice shrill and squeaky, she rasped, "Sometimes I'm hungry."

"A glutton is what you are!" he shouted. "Edith! No bread for Natalie at mealtimes. And no chocolate cake for dessert," he added, walking away.

Natalie ran to the front garden to get away from the house, but even the scent of the tea roses on either side of the driveway failed to diminish her anger. That evening, she discovered the Skinnies had invited a Swiss couple to dinner. Edith, a hand behind her back, passed the basket of rolls around the table. The grown-ups talked and laughed amongst themselves, as if she weren't there. When Edith passed Natalie, she automatically placed a roll on Natalie's salad plate. Edith must have forgotten Skinno's orders.

At breakfast the next day, Skinno convinced Skinna that Natalie must attend Remedial Summer School in the village. It was very unfair of Skinno, because Natalie was a very good student who didn't need remedial classes. Remedial school had started the last week of April and was to last till the end of August. All during that time, she would miss visiting Papa in the mornings.

From the hallway, Natalie heard him say, "She's idle, which means she'll soon be up to mischief. Children need a disciplined life."

"I won't go," Natalie insisted. "If I go, I won't see Papa in the morning."

She repeated her argument so often that Skinna offered her a brief second visit to Papa to wish him good night before she went to bed. But Skinno was adamant. Natalie must attend Remedial Summer School.

Chapter 20

Remedial School

Two days later, Tante Pauline took Natalie to her first day of Summer school. Before she left, Skinna pointed to a room down the hall where about twenty boys and girls waited, each behind a desk. Natalie went towards the room and observed them from the threshold. Some children seemed no older than six-years-old, and the tallest boy, whom others called Hans, looked around fifteen. When the teacher called the children's names, they answered, "yes" or "here," before sitting down.

Natalie, seated at the corner front desk, stood up without saying anything, humiliated to be twelve years old in a class with six-year-old little ones and a few older children. After telling them to sit down, Mademoiselle Jacquenot asked each child, in turn to read a paragraph from a book she chose.

The worst reader was Hans, the tall blond boy, who mumbled so much that no one understood what he read. Natalie read last, clearly, without hesitation or mistakes, from Jules Vernes, *Around the World in Eighty Days*.

Mademoiselle Jacquenot said, "Well done, Natalie! All of you should aim to read as well as Natalie. There is plenty of room for improvement in this class. Then she said, "Now, let's tackle some arithmetic."

The children bent over their slates, busy with subtraction and division. The first few were easy. Then came harder ones. Natalie wrote down the problems and found the answers, but the teacher didn't call on her again. Instead, she called on Hans.

"Where is your slate, Hans?"

"No need," he replied. The teacher just nodded when he gave her all the right answers. She moved on to other children, many of whom had trouble carrying numbers forward or placing decimal points. She handed Natalie sheets of paper and asked her to help the younger children. Natalie did her best. She was glad to be useful, almost happy, and besides, she had something good to tell Papa.

Within days, she had become the teacher's assistant, erasing the blackboard for her, carrying messages to and from the principal's office, arranging books in alphabetical order, writing down in the register the titles of books on loan opposite the name of borrowers. The teacher also left Natalie free to read any book she chose.

Was that why the children disliked her? They skipped her turn when they played jump rope, and never chose her for team games. Surely it was not because she could read? Although in Montreux, no horrid kids called her a *Yid,* a *Youpine*, or a dirty Jew, it was as bad. The oldest boy, Hans, who was in fact fifteen years old and bossy, ran after her at noon break, calling her a refugee.

Natalie protested, her face hot, "I'm not a refugee. I live with my family, Monsieur and Madame Charles."

"Madame Charles has no children," Hans countered.

Children gathered around them.

"She's my aunt. My Papa's there too."

He snickered. "Must be that old refugee that gets so drunk, the postman has to drag him home."

It was a lie, of course, but Natalie didn't know what to say. She ran home along a street where shadows hid and pressed hard against the trees for comfort, while her own shadow kept on breaking into pieces as she advanced.

That afternoon, not wanting to worry Papa by saying that Hans was mean, and that she wondered where Maman was hiding, Natalie asked, "We won't stay in Montreux much longer, will we?"

"But it's such a lovely place!" A bout of coughing interrupted him. "Don't you like the beach by the lake?"

"Yes," she answered truthfully, "but there is no sand and no parasol and my feet hurt on the pebbles."

"Yes," Papa agreed, "It's hard on your feet at first. But you know that the beach in France you remember so well with the sand and the parasol is just on the other side of the lake?" He picked up a pencil from his bedside table. On a sheet of paper, he drew a lake between two countries and continued drawing. He explained that there were pebbles on the beach in France as well, but that her grandparents had sand delivered each year to be spread around their beach cabin. On his drawing pad, there was now a parasol above tiny people on the French shore, waving to tiny people on the other shore, who held red flags with a white cross in the middle. The beach had a million pebbles on the Swiss side.

"Here is something I drew," Natalie announced. She handed him her drawing of a mouse. Papa promised to ask Oncle Marc to take her mouse drawing to Maman. "I have something else too," said Natalie. She pulled the blue good luck stone she had saved for him. It had lost all color. Natalie could feel tears coming.

"I'm sure that if you wet it, it will get blue again," Papa suggested. Papa knew everything.

She licked the stone and handed it to him, topped now by a circle of bluishness.

He blew her a kiss. "I'll keep it as long as I live, as a souvenir of this afternoon with you," he said.

Natalie stood straight and happy.

"When you stand like this, you remind me of your Maman," Papa said.

"But I want to be like you."

"Believe me, you don't."

"Yes, yes, I do." She nodded several times.

Papa coughed. "You are getting bigger and stronger every day."

"You are getting stronger every day too, Papa."

Just then, Oncle Marc appeared in the doorway and Papa beckoned him in.

"Yes, *Chérie*, of course. Now, it's time for my medication. Run down and see if there is fruit juice in the kitchen for me, and find Pierre and ask if he has any fresh apples."

Happy to help, Natalie glided down the hall, and the stairs, on the soles of her new blue felt slippers. The kitchen was empty because Edith was away until four o'clock. She decided to go first to the back garden where Pierre was picking apples. Going out the kitchen door and down the stairs, Natalie was careful not to ruin her new slippers on the walk to the fruit trees.

Natalie was returning to the kitchen with two juicy apples that Pierre had given her as Skinno came down the back stairs toward her looking angry. "Where have you been? Get back to your father with the juice!" he hissed, and hurried off. Natalie didn't care about Skinno. She had a sweet treat for Papa!

In the kitchen, Natalie put on a small apron and dropped an apple in each pocket. Turning to the get the juice she noticed the rubbish bin stood in a corner with its lid partially off. Inside, something bright caught Natalie's eye. Her drawing of the mouse with the thin tail, crumpled. It was her best, the one she'd saved for Maman! A lump grew at the back of her tongue. Skinno was the meanest man in the world. But Papa was waiting for her.

Her face burning, Natalie found the fruit juice and managed to carry the small jug, with an inverted glass on top, upstairs. Papa was in his bathroom, drinking out of his toothbrush tumbler.

"You took your pills," she exclaimed.

"No-no, not yet," Papa said, closing the bathroom door.

Back in bed, tumbler in hand, he counted four white pills. Natalie handed Papa the jug. When he was done, he set the pitcher on his crowded bedside table. The glass, too close to the edge, toppled, but Natalie, hovering by the foot of the bed, caught it.

"Good catch," Papa said, turning to the wall.

Natalie took the tumbler to the bathroom. Whatever was left in the glass stung her eyes. It smelled of rotten apples, or what was left in wine glasses after dinner with guests. She sniffed the glass once, unable to understand why grown-ups enjoyed wine with its vile smell. She rinsed Papa's tumbler, letting the water run a long time.

After dinner, it was time to say good night and the ritual "thank you," before going to her room. Natalie put on her pajamas and, from habit, slipped her hand under her pillow. A lump met her hand. She pulled it out to find a fresh roll wrapped in a flowered handkerchief. She chewed it slowly, tasting each sweet mouthful as if it were cake. Only Edith could have done this. Edith was on her side, then, against mean old Skinno.

Chapter 21

A Kiss

After lunch that Saturday, Skinna said, "Go on, Natalie. Time for your nap."

Natalie lingered on the stairs. She wasn't a baby. She would soon be twelve, and didn't need a nap. Even Lilla had stopped taking naps ages ago. Instead, Natalie spied on Skinna who was visiting Papa. It was easy from the outer stairs, linking the lower and upper balcony, to look inside Papa's room, reflected in the open French windows. Or, standing against the wall just beyond the corner, to peer in and see the room inside the large wall mirror.

"Poor little one, she thinks I'm getting better," Papa said, his head on the pillows.

Skinna, arranging branches in a vase, took a step back. The stems drew swirls in the water.

"Who says you're not?" her voice was bright, like the green ferns on her dress.

"No one is fooling me. Not even your doctor. I only wish I knew how long—"

"No-no" Skinna spoke fast. "You mustn't speak like that. I chose these branches especially for you. Three chestnuts on this side, and there, a butterfly floats by. Lots of good things waiting for you."

"Lots indeed. A butterfly and a chaise longue."

"And you have me."

Her voice was strange and intense. Skinna spun around and bent over Papa. She kissed him on the lips. She wasn't Papa's wife! How dare she kiss him, when she won't let me touch him? Natalie wanted to run in and shout that Skinna was bad. Skinna had given her the Heidi book, chocolates and almond truffles. Natalie had felt warmer toward her. Now, this had to happen.

"Has it occurred to you, Pauline, that if I were hale and hearty, you wouldn't think of me?" Papa asked gently.

Skinna tightened her fingers around a spiky green chestnut.

Papa didn't say what Skinna wanted to hear. Papa should have slapped Skinna's face, so that Natalie could burst in and see Skinna forced to run out.

"You should have children, Pauline," Papa said.

"Marc never wanted any. He's not really married to me. He's married to his research, in Paris, as well as here. He keeps making excuses. At first, it was 'after my promotion' and then it was wait for his next promotion. Last year, a younger man was promoted ahead of him, and ever since..."

Natalie retreated, puzzled and upset.

Chapter 22

Cages

When the doctor came to see Papa, Natalie sometimes accompanied Pierre to the shops to pick up parcels and art supplies from the post office for Papa. One day in early July, on the way back with Pierre, Natalie noticed a narrow box sticking out of a paper bag among the packages in the crate at her feet.

"Pierre?" she asked. "That one without a label, is it for me?"

"That one's mine. I'll take care of it," he said, keeping his eyes on the road.

"What's inside?"

"Oh, little things that might break," Pierre said.

"How do you know?" She wriggled in her seat. "What little things might break?"

"Well," Pierre said, "things like eyeglasses and whatnots."

They reached the back door. Pierre let Natalie bring in the books and magazines, but he carried the box of whatnots on top of the larger, heavier crate.

Occasionally, before their shopping excursions, they stopped at Skinno's lab, where the attendant let Natalie feed the rabbits and hold the guinea pigs. Natalie felt very sad for them.

One afternoon, as they walked back to the car, she suddenly stopped on the sidewalk. "Pierre," Natalie said, "I left my cardigan in the lab."

"Don't dawdle," he warned.

She ran back inside while he waited in the car, parked by the door of the building. Skinno would never figure out what she was about to do.

In the front of each guinea pig cage was a door. But at the back, a common panel kept all the cages shut, with just two horizontal sliding rods. Natalie tugged at a rod till it gradually moved toward her and slipped out of its rail. Soon, she stood both rods in the corner, glimpsing the guinea pigs, mice, and rabbits pressed against the walls of their cages. She quickly opened the window, grabbed her cardigan, and ran out, slamming the door shut behind her.

During the night, Natalie dreamt that an endless stream of animals ran into the forest, melting into its greenness, and though she was watching from the rooftop of her home in France, she was at the same time playing with the rabbits, while feeding them carrots. They spoke to her in words she later couldn't remember. In the morning, as she lay half-awake in bed, the door flew open.

"Let me go! Put me down, Natalie screamed, as she was carried down to the whitewashed basement. Skinno, tight-lipped, stood her up. In one motion, he stripped her of her pajama bottoms, which he threw in the black entrance of an empty doghouse. Holding her firmly from around her back, he steadied his right foot on an apple crate, then pulled her facedown over his bent knee. There, between piles of logs, neat shelves of mountain honey, and rows of gardening tools, Skinno spanked her hard, like a machine set to run till the end of the world.

"A monster, you're a monster, do you hear?" he repeated.

Initially, Natalie cried out, but soon she held her breath. Each time Skinno's hand fell with a burning slap, she tried to hear in her head a song Pierre sang when he did the weeding. To help herself ignore the beating, she repeated the small part she knew, *La-haut sur la montagne*: "High up on the mountain."

Skinno let go. Natalie could barely stand up, her nakedness nearly as severe a disgrace as the spanking.

"What are you singing?" he demanded.

Retreating, hands spread over her lower tummy, Natalie gasped, "*La-Haut*."

"I'll give you songs! Apologize, you wretch!" he demanded. His hand went up again, and his face beaded with sweat.

She apologized.

He left.

Natalie stayed in the basement until Edith came and helped her into her pajamas, which worsened the burning on her bottom. Edith half-carried her upstairs to bathe, but Natalie was unable to climb into the tub. Edith sponged Natalie as she stood trembling, and spread a special cream all over her back. Natalie was numb, but still could not sit down, and had to sleep on her tummy.

The next morning, Skinno opened her door. A hand on the knob, without looking at her, he declared, "I won't upset your father by telling him about your low behavior. I told him you have a fever. You'll stay in your room for three days. That will give you time to reflect on your despicable act."

Early the next morning, Edith was on her hands and knees waxing the floor of the bathroom when Natalie heard Skinno say, "From now on, Edith, she is to eat her meals in the kitchen." Skinna must have been listening with her door open, because Natalie heard high heels clicking away down the corridor. Natalie hoped no one would guess what a relief eating in the kitchen was going to be. That evening, for the first time, Natalie went to the kitchen for supper. In his overalls, hands around a glass of red wine, Pierre stood by the tiled stove, listening to Edith, whose round white arms lay on either side of her plate.

"Children are a trial, I grant you," she was saying, "all the same, he went too far. Oh! Speaking of the devil, there you are! Come and tell Tante Edie all about it."

"Tante Edie!" Natalie was in friendly territory, then. Her eyes downcast, she explained that the mice and rabbits and guinea pigs in the stinking lab could not get out. Now it was easy to cry.

"Monsieur says it's at least two hundred francs down the drain," Edith said. "Last night, when the caretaker came to lock up, he found the little things running wild, only a few in their cages. A mess! Glad I didn't have to clean up," she told Pierre. "Could never stand mice."

Pierre said, "Why don't you give the child something to eat?"

Natalie ate creamy rice pudding with purple stewed cherries on top. Edith brought her a slice of pink ham with a hill of potato salad. "I ate dessert first. That is fun. They would never let me do that in the dining room," she said.

Edith and Pierre exchanged a look.

"I don't know that they've got all the creatures back," said Edith. "And Pierre, the lights are off again in the bathroom and the upstairs landing. She's been asking."

Pierre picked up his box of tools and a basket with small boxes in it. What did it mean, that the bathroom lights were off again? Would Pierre bring things to Papa? Natalie remembered the smell in Papa's mug, which she rinsed out in the bathroom. But no, Pierre would not bring horrid stuff for Papa to drink!

Chapter 23

Surprises

From his lounge chair on the balcony, a traveling rug tucked around his legs, Papa inspected Natalie, who waited at the door. "I like your hair coiled like telephone receivers on your ears," he said.

Natalie was shifting from one foot to the other, anxiously wondering whether Papa knew about the cages.

With laughing wrinkles about his eyes, Papa said, "To show that I missed you, I've prepared a little surprise for you." He pointed to a box wrapped in paper near the door.

He wasn't angry! So, he didn't know what she had done. They looked at each other expectantly. She tore into the parcel. Inside the box was a blue rucksack, new and stiff, with many pockets.

It seemed like Christmas, when it was all right to drop wrapping paper all over the floor, and they had the best time with Papa, who'd made them gifts and sang about angels in the countryside. Natalie plunged her hands into the rucksack pockets and threw papers and ribbons to the floor to discover a compass, chocolates with hazelnut, pictures, and a small pad of paper with a pencil attached. Inside of a small leather pouch was a pocketknife with two blades, and a tiny pair of scissors in the shape of a Heron, its beak opening as she worked the scissors open and pulling back inside the handle when she closed them. There was also an Alpine flower book.

"Can we go on a picnic, the two of us, please Papa, please?" She inclined her head to her shoulder.

He only said, "Go on, there's something else."

She discovered the best gift rolled into a cardboard tube. It was a map, her very own Map Game. Papa had thought of everything. Villages and fences, boulders, border guards, trolleys, streams and flowers, each appeared behind a name-bearing placard, planted inside a tuft of grass. Pierre was on the map, in a checkered shirt, hoeing. Two snails progressed companionably under a cherry tree. There were flags on either side of the Franco-Swiss border, and a red fox cub peered out of his den. Maman waved from an upstairs window in France. Perhaps she was safe. Natalie said nothing.

"You must tell me whether I made mistakes," Papa said seriously. "I made it to scale. A map must be accurate, you see, or it's no good."

She couldn't tell him.

"Is it the snails? Too hot for them this time of day?"

"I think they'd be out, but..." she trailed off.

Papa waited. Hanging her head as if it were her fault, Natalie murmured, "The bridge." There was no bridge. She couldn't bear to look at Papa.

"Tell you what, we've got to put a bridge or two over that stream," Papa declared in a soothing voice, before his cough interrupted him.

"This is the best map in the whole world," Natalie declared.

"Do you like maps?"

"I only like your maps. We have maps at school, without pictures. They're very hard to read."

"Those are maps for grown-ups. Still, maps and plans are very important, Nat. They show you how to prepare a trip."

"Even when there are no words?"

"Even without words. A map shows how far you need to walk, where there is danger, where there is water to drink, where there are towns and villages. There are also maps showing street names and how to go from one place to another. There are all kinds of maps. The main thing to remember is that they tell you about your journey and keep you safe, away from nasty dogs and mean guards." Papa lay back against his pillows and closed his eyes. Natalie was wondering whether she should leave on tiptoes so he could nap, when he smiled. "Natalie, *Papagena*, please pick up those wrappers from the floor."

Natalie rolled them into a ball and went to the bathroom to dump them into the wastepaper basket. At the bottom of the wastebasket sat the cover from the narrow parcel Pierre had brought. Was it a box of light bulbs? She was about to ask Papa when the doctor walked in, carrying his black bag. She had to leave, but not before pressing her treasures to her chest.

From then on, Natalie wore her rucksack everywhere. She filled it with Papa's old slippers, her books, and a smallish log for the fireplace, the only one that fit into her rucksack. She talked with Papa more about the map details, and found out how long it would take to hike over the mountains into France, how often people needed to rest, how many snacks, how much money to take. She wished she'd taken her own French money, hidden in her chest of drawers at home.

She hummed Pierre's songs now that Skinno was back in France. She needed money. From Skinna's many purses,

Natalie stole Swiss coins and hid them in the foil from her teatime chocolate bars. She stored the wrapped coins inside the leather holder of her Swiss knife.

"Papa, do you love everybody?" she asked one day.

"Just about." He was sharpening a pencil with a penknife, making the point very thin and sharp.

"I hate some people," Natalie said, flitting about, unable to settle. Sometimes she hated Maman, but felt guilty. Mostly, she hated Skinno and, because Skinna had kissed Papa, she hated her too, though she was nicer, especially when Skinno was away.

"You only think you do because some girl got better grades at school or someone received more presents. But if you try, you'll find that you love them after all," he said. He stopped drawing during a moment of coughing and frowning, and then resumed, concentrating on shading a large area.

"How do you try?" she asked.

"The same as with everything else, Nat. Practice. You practiced reading and writing and riding a bicycle and swimming. Eventually, you knew how to ride and read and write and swim. It's the same for everything. If you plan and practice loving with all your heart, you will succeed."

"Always?" Natalie pulled on her fingers to make them crack.

"It gets easier. You'll see. But only if you practice," he said, winking at her as if to say many more things. He lowered his sketch pad onto his lap and leaned back against his pillows. He had drawn a bird with one wing showing, not flying yet. There was a lovely curved wedge of fanned feathers at the tip of the single wing. Perhaps he would draw the other wing later. She guessed that for reasons only grown-ups knew, there might not be another wing.

She waited for Papa to pick up his pencil. He wasn't like her. He was good. He loved everybody. He'd practiced a long time. To be good like him, she was willing to practice. Yet she balked at the thought of loving Skinno.

"Papa?" she asked.

"Yes, Natalie."

"Will you sing, 'Angels in the Countryside'?"

He sighed. "On your birthday, I will. I have to save my breath today."

Natalie hoped that Skinno would not be back for her twelfth birthday.

Chapter 24

Lost Homes

Skinna always did what Papa wanted. Natalie wondered whether her aunt's house with a view of the lake had become Papa's home. She asked him one afternoon, "Is this your home now?"

"I feel at home here," Papa said. "This was Pauline's parents' home. When they died, it became hers."

Natalie thought of the Gregorys. "My friend Rosie Gregory had a home near my school, on Rue des Frênes, but the Germans stole that house from the family, and they chopped down the trees around it. It doesn't look the same anymore, and Rosie's gone, so now she has no home."

"Rosie will always have her home."

"She will? Where?"

"It's a secret." He coughed a small repeated cough.

"So you won't tell me?"

Papa smiled. "It's a secret, but I'll share it with you."

Natalie moved closer.

Papa said, "I agree that without trees, that house doesn't look the same anymore. Still, there's always a place where a home is safe."

"Where?" Natalie asked.

"Inside you. You can go there whenever you want in your memory. Nobody can take that away from you. That's the best part."

It was a sad answer. If you had a home, you could run up the stairs to your room, or sit at the dining room table, or slide down the banister, or lie on the rug to read. You could play hide-and-seek in it. How could a home be inside somebody? It would have to be smaller than the tiniest dollhouse, and you could never run inside. Natalie felt very miserable. She had lost Rosie, but she still had Papa. Even if she remembered in her mind what he was like, in real life, Papa was not home with her and Maman and her sisters. He was not with her all the time, as he was before that horrid war. She couldn't bring herself to tell Papa that she had no idea where Rosie, her mother, and her brother had gone, so that she had no friend left. Instead she asked, "Where is Maman?"

"She's in a quiet, very good place. For a while longer."

"But where?"

"I don't know that," Papa said reasonably, "but I'm sure nothing bad will happen to your lovely Maman."

"Do you send letters?" Natalie peered over his pad to see the sketch in progress.

"Of course." He brushed away erasure bits with the heel of his hand. They rolled like grains of sand to the bedspread.

"But you can't send a letter if you don't have an address," Natalie pointed out.

Papa continued to draw, his pencil making tiny, *tov-tov* scooting sounds when he made short strokes. "There is Marc and the Red Cross and friends."

Papa didn't know what awful Skinno had done to her drawings. Should she tell him? She decided against it, because Skinno might have thrown out Papa's letters to Maman, too. Skinno had arrived two days before, and was going back to France in ten days. Natalie would be happier. Her latest drawings waited inside her rucksack.

Chapter 25

A Secret

Natalie had not told Skinna that there was no school on Thursday or Saturday mornings. After breakfast as usual, she walked toward the school with her book bag. The grass was wet with dew and she longed for somewhere warm and dry to sit, feeling unhappy about having nowhere to go. If the school was open, and someone asked why she'd come, she would say she wanted to return some books and choose new ones from the little room they called the library, where she could sit and read undisturbed.

Someone behind her made her jump by sneezing loudly, "like the trumpets of Jericho," as she and Hélène liked to say. When she turned around, she found Hans, the lanky blond boy with rumpled clothes, holding a white bag in his hand. He was smiling, friendly for once. A welcome change.

"Forgot there is no school today?" he asked. He pulled a raisin roll out of the bag, held it between his teeth, and offered her the open bag. He managed to say, "Hef yarsef, Nat'lie."

The sun was shining now, already warm, wiping away the dew. The smell rising from the paper bag, yeasty and sweet, was impossible to resist. Natalie took out a roll. "Thank you," she said, "we only get these on Sundays."

"Let's go to my aunt's place," Hans suggested.

Natalie wished she could reply that her aunt would welcome them too, but she knew better. "Will your aunt be all right with us coming in?" she asked.

"She's gone to Lausanne with my mother. They're looking for fancy hats. We can sit in the back on her lawn chairs."

After a short walk from the school, below the slight hill just a few turns away from the Skinnies's house, Hans opened a side door to a garden. It was full of orange trumpet vines, lilies, and pansies, set around a chalk-white, two-storied villa that had bricks around the windows, and closed, pale blue shutters hiding the rooms. They sat under an umbrella, facing the lake and vineyards, munching on rolls.

"Why do you always carry books?" Hans asked, stretching his long frame on a lounge chair, his hands behind his head. "What are you reading?"

"It's called, *Twenty Thousand Leagues Under the Sea*," replied Natalie. "I borrowed it from school. It's about an underwater boat."

"A submarine! Read some to me, okay?"

"I've finished it. You can have it," she said, handing him the volume.

Hans didn't take it. "No. It hurts my eyes."

"If you read me a page, I'll read you a page," said Natalie. "You'll see it's really, really good. There's a captain Nemo—that means 'nobody' in Latin, Papa told me. He's bad, but in the end might have changed."

Hans picked up the book and brought the first page close to his nose. Natalie thought he did it for fun. Then, he started slowly to read, but he was interrupted by explosive sneezes. He whipped out a large handkerchief to wipe his face. When he stuffed it back into his pocket, his eyes were red. Natalie asked, "Your mother. Why didn't she take you with her to Lausanne?"

"I've been there. Just lots of old buildings. I'd be bored stiff looking at hats. That's not what boys like to do," he answered.

"But then, who cooks dinner for you?"

"The cook comes in to make my meals. I like beef and lamb with *roesti*."

"What is that?"

"You've never heard of *roesti*? You, a girl from France? I thought you knew everything," he teased. "*Roesti* is grated potatoes that you fry as a cake until it's crisp. You dump grated cheese on top. Delicious!" He licked two fingers of one hand, dipped them into the bottom of the paper bag, and licked the crumbs off.

"You spoke about your Papa," Hans said suddenly, "What about your mother? Is she in Montreux?"

"She couldn't come because she doesn't have a passport," Natalie said. She didn't want to tell Hans that Maman was a Jew. "What about your own Papa. Why isn't he here with you?"

"I'll tell you a secret." Bending from his chair to hers, Hans put his hands around her left ear,

"He's a war hero. He won medals."

"How come? Switzerland is not at war," Natalie whispered back.

"That's what the newspapers say. But my father's busy helping people in danger."

"You mean, he helps them cross the border?" she asked. She remembered the boy who helped her and Skinna slip under barbed wire at the border. "That's dangerous!"

"That's why he isn't home much. He has a carbine. He loaned it to me. I've used it twice to hunt," he boasted. "I promised not to tell anyone."

"You told me."

"Because you're safe. You're a friend, and friends help each other, right?" He cocked his head, letting his blond hair fall over his right ear.

"Right," she said flatly.

"Where do you live, Natalie?"

She told him.

"Not far. Race you there," said Hans. Abandoning his lounge chair, he dashed out of the garden. Natalie got up and remembered to pick up her book bag, to let him win. He was already too far for her to catch up to him, but she ran anyway.

He waited proudly under a linden tree, his face pink. "I won."

"You gave me too little notice," Natalie said, breathing harder than she needed, to shame him. She heard the noon bell ring at a church. "*A bientôt*! I must go in, or I'll be late for lunch."

On Thursday, going down to breakfast, Natalie found Papa up and dressed, in the corridor. His clothes drooped on him. He was unsteady, and took slow steps, leaning on Skinno and Skinna, who walked on either side, supporting him.

Natalie ran and stopped short in front of him. "Where are you going? Please don't leave me," she cried.

"We're taking your Papa to see a different doctor, a very good one, in Geneva. We might be back tonight. But if Papa is tired, we'll come back tomorrow," Skinna announced.

Papa smiled without letting go of Skinna's arm. He gave Natalie a little wave with one hand.

"Come back soon! Don't leave me!" Natalie begged, heavy-hearted, watching the trio go toward the stairs.

"I'll never leave you," Papa said, taking the first step down the stairs.

From the hallway, Natalie watched them get into the car waiting in the drive. Skinno helped Papa raise his feet into the back of the car, while Skinna arranged pillows behind him. Then Skinna got in and slammed her door shut, and the Skinnies drove away with Papa, leaving her behind.

Why did no one tell her Papa was going to Geneva? Was it a secret? Everybody had secrets. Well, she had a secret too. Natalie thought about this during breakfast, as she chewed the corners of toast with plum jam, and drank half a glass of milk. Then, for the second day in a row, she left as if going to school, only today she was feeling miserable. She was relieved to see Hans walk toward her from the end of the street. Hans had talked about teaching her to play checkers. If they played, she might forget about Papa being away for a while.

They walked side by side without talking until Hans pulled out a small, carved box.

"What's that?" Natalie asked.

"You've never seen chess pieces?" he asked back.

They were dainty, strange little things. "Where did you get them?"

"My father made them for me out of ivory. He's good with his hands. Look," he pulled out a box as large as two matchboxes. "That's where I keep my chess pieces. They have pegs underneath to fit into tiny holes on the board, so they don't get lost. This is the horse, and this is a bishop, and this one's a castle. I like the horse the best."

"Is it hard to learn?"

"It's tricky. Let's start with checkers. It's easier. The pieces are all the same, one color for each player. I'll set up the game." From his shirt pocket, he pulled a small checkerboard folded into four and opened it. "Two players. We use only the dark squares. Let's play at the church. It's quiet there."

"My Papa is good with his hands too," Natalie said, walking alongside Hans. "But mostly he draws now because he has to stay in bed."

They found the church door open and walked into the meeting room. There was no one around. They sat at the corner of a table, where Hans began to set up his checkerboard with the pawns.

Head bent over the board he asked, "What's wrong with your father? Is he paralyzed?"

"No, but it's hard for him to breathe," Natalie answered.

"You can only move on the diagonal," Hans explained. "The first one to get to the back row across the board gets a queen—a pawn on top of another. That means he'll win."

Natalie asked, "Why is it a queen and not a king?"

"Because—I don't know. Because women are so bossy."

Natalie kept quiet, but she didn't agree. Skinna always let Skinno make decisions, even in Skinna's own house in Montreux. Skinna had done it in their Paris flat too, she remembered.

They played a couple of games, which Hans won. "You're no fun," he declared. "You do the first thing that comes into your head, so your pieces are too easy to take prisoner. You need a plan."

"A plan? What kind of a plan?"

"You need to think about what will happen when you make a move. Try and guess what I might do. Never get all your pieces in a clump in the middle of the board."

They tried again. And again. Hans won each time. Natalie didn't like to lose, but she hoped to soon learn and win some of the time.

"How come you play?" Natalie asked.

"My father taught me. He's a world champion at chess as well," Hans said proudly.

Natalie had no idea whether Papa could win against Hans's father. She wanted to say that Papa was a French champion. But it didn't sound as good as world champion. But it seemed unfair that Hans should win every time. "My Papa taught me to draw."

"Show me. Draw me your house. I'll tell you whether it's any good," Hans said.

On a crumpled sheet of paper, Natalie drew Skinna's house, with four windows on either side of the door, and eight windows upstairs, and more on the upper floor, and the alley with rose bushes in front. She didn't draw the back of the house with the balconies. "How is that?"

"Not bad," Hans conceded. "Is your room at the front of the house? Yes?"

She nodded.

"Which one?"

Natalie pointed to the right end window on the third floor. "Papa's is on the second floor, at the corner to the right. He has two windows."

Someone opened a door; they heard footsteps.

Hans said, "Time to stretch our legs. Let's go to the market."

They left the meeting room quietly, hearing music from the harmonium cascading into the empty church sanctuary. But Natalie didn't want to go to the market in case she came face to face with Edith looking for button mushrooms, or greengages, those golden-green plums, to bottle, or large trays of raspberries to turn into jam.

"I don't want to go," she told Hans.

"Then wait here. I'll be back," he said.

Alone in the common room, Natalie wondered what to say if someone asked what she was doing in the church. Listening to the music that would accompany the psalms, she wished she'd been given music lessons so that she could play Skinna's piano.

Hans returned out of breath, carrying a basket the size of a football, covered by a blue and green dishcloth. "Let's go," he said.

Natalie said, "You should get a bicycle. Then, you wouldn't get so winded when you're in a hurry."

"Nah," he said, shaking his head. His hair fell over his eyes till he pushed it away. "I want a motorcycle. My dad promised me one for my birthday. I'll be thirteen, then."

She raised a shoulder. "You're not old enough. I mean, to get a license."

"But my father is! Come, I've got something that can't wait in this basket."

"Show me," she urged, craning her neck.

He raised a corner of the towel.

"Cherries! I love them," exclaimed Natalie. "Did you buy them?"

"What do you think?" He lowered the cloth. "Some things are meant just for us."

They walked to a bench on the square and ate handfuls of juicy red, shiny cherries, that tasted like lemon, and quince, and orange, and smelled like wine, only better. They sat spitting the pits on the grass all around them, laughing. When the basket was empty, Hans pushed it with the pretty dishcloth on top into the trash bin at the gate. What a waste, Natalie thought, without rescuing the basket or the dishcloth.

She looked at the clock tower of the church. "I'm going home," she announced. She had fun, but she wanted to be neat and tidy with her hair brushed in case Papa came home that evening.

Chapter 26

The Intruder

The following Friday Hans mentioned that the next day in the morning he wanted to go to the Chillon Castle, a chateau built on the tiny island in the lake. Natalie didn't have a chance to respond because he was soon surrounded by a noisy group of boys.

On Sunday, Natalie met Skinna and Skinno in the entryway as they were returning from church. She noticed Skinna wearing a new hat with a lilac veil, and Skinno was dressed in a dark suit with a perfect white shirt. They were hanging their coats in the hallway closet when angry voices irrupted from the kitchen.

"What is going on?" Skinno demanded, turning towards the kitchen, whipping his glasses off his nose with one hand.

Pierre was backing into the hall, dragging someone who was trying to wriggle free. Natalie was stunned to see it was Hans.

"*Excusez-moi*!" said Pierre. "Madame and Monsieur, I found this boy prowling upstairs just minutes ago," he explained.

Hans's blond hair was askew, and his blue- checkered shirt hung half out of his shorts. He broke free from Pierre and jumped up, tucking his shirttails back into his shorts and pushing the unruly hair off his forehead. Glancing at Natalie, he pursed his mouth and gave dusting taps to his clothes.

"Prowling, did you say? Upstairs?" Skinno asked, one eyebrow raised. "Where, upstairs?"

"On the second floor, Monsieur. The boy was walking ahead of me down the corridor. I had gone upstairs to ask Monsieur Francis whether he wanted his lunch tray."

"Thank you, Pierre. Take your afternoon off," said Skinno. When the kitchen door closed, with exaggerated politeness, Skinno asked Hans, "To what do we owe the pleasure of this unexpected intrusion?"

Hans squared his shoulders. He smiled. "*Voila.* It's quite simple. Natalie told me to come.

She can't keep up at school, see, or do her homework, because she can hardly read. I was looking for her to help her with her reading. The teacher told me to." He gave Natalie a wink.

"Not true!" she burst out, hot with resentment.

"Go on," Skinno, chin up, told Hans.

Natalie wanted to speak, but Skinno raised his right hand like a policeman to stop her.

"She pretends to read, you see. But she only looks at the pictures," Hans said. "Perhaps you noticed. She even holds her book upside down sometimes."

Natalie was furious. She'd only once held her book upside down to show Hans the caption under a picture of the *Nautilus* in *Twenty Thousand Leagues Under the Sea.*

Skinna just stood back, patting the back of her hair. Hans rolled his shoulders. Natalie danced from one foot to the other, anxious to set things straight.

Skinno looked like a bull. He forced a laugh as he said, "That's a good one! Would you by any chance be talking about yourself? I've heard Natalie read, and I assure you she needs no remedial help, from a German Swiss at that!" It wasn't true that Skinno had heard her read, but he often saw her reading in the house. "Natalie may have problems," he went on, "but reading isn't one of them. She reads as well as I do. As for you, my boy, I've heard about your talents. I must ask you to empty your pockets."

"All I have is my handkerchief and an eraser," Hans retorted, opening empty palms.

"Do as you're told," ordered Skinno.

Hans extracted a pink eraser from his pocket.

"You left something behind."

"Yes, but that's a present from Natalie." Hans grinned.

Skinno took a step closer to Hans. Between his teeth, he said, "Let's see that present."

Hans pulled out the ivory letter opener with an elephant under a palm tree that used to lie on the sitting room bureau. Skinno picked it up. He turned it over twice. Facing Natalie, who stared in disbelief, he asked, "Did you give this to Hans?"

"I did not!" she shouted with indignation.

Skinno growled, "You, little bastard, are a thief."

"*Ecoutez*," Hans said. "Natalie wanted me to meet her father. Since nobody opened the door when I rang the front bell, I came in through the back, looking for her."

Skinno pounced. "Natalie's father is too ill for visitors. Those who go into his room might catch his disease."

"You cannot catch heart disease from someone else, you see," Hans declared disdainfully, a hand on his hip, as if explaining something difficult to an ignorant man.

"Who told you it was his heart?" asked Skinno.

"I said Papa had trouble breathing," Natalie murmured.

At that point, Hans had an explosive sneezing fit. He

tore a handkerchief out of his pocket. Out of it, something shiny bounced onto the parquet floor by Skinna's feet. She bent down fast and picked it up before Hans could. In Skinna's hand lay a silver cufflink topped by a blue stone scarab.

"Now for the other one," she ordered, adopting Skinno's icy tone.

"They had fallen off the chest of drawers. I was going to hand them to your maid for you," Hans said. His cocky smile was gone.

"Empty both pockets," Skinno ordered.

The second cufflink appeared. This time, Skinna picked it up with her lacy handkerchief and examined it as if she'd never seen it.

"The other pocket again," Skinno instructed.

Hans shrugged.

Skinno advanced and Hans took a step back, but could not retreat further because he stood against the wall of the hallway.

"Do you need help, by any chance?" Skinno offered menacingly.

As if his shoulders were sore or his fingers too stiff, Hans took a long time before producing Skinna's favorite brooch, the gold one, encircling three pearls lined up on a pointy leaf.

"This too had fallen," Hans began.

"Nothing fell, and you never intended to hand anything to the maid. Turn both pockets inside out. Now. Or I'll call the police," Skinno roared,

"Pauline, get the phone book and find the number, will you!"

Skinna left to get the phone book.

From the second pocket of his shorts, Hans brought

out the red leather case with the bird-shaped scissors, a nail file, and a suede-covered nail buff that Skinna used when she buffed her nails.

"Who put you up to this? Your mother?"

"No," Hans muttered, and Natalie saw him flinch.

"What would she do if I took you home to tell her?" Skinno threatened.

Hans cringed and answered so low that Natalie could barely hear. "She'll use the belt."

Skinno crossed his arms and pushed Hans with humiliating questions. "I've looked into your background since neighbors reported trouble and we've heard rumors. Your father abandoned your mother without a single franc, before you were born, isn't that so?" He didn't wait for an answer. "You never met him. Your mother came back to Montreux from Zurich with you as a baby, looking for work. She's been scrubbing floors and taking in laundry to feed you and keep a roof over your head. This is how you repay her?" he thundered.

"I only took small things," Hans muttered.

Natalie found it hard to absorb what she heard. What if Hans had really meant to meet her and Papa? Perhaps all the trouble was her fault, since she'd told Hans which window was Papa's room and which was hers. By drawing Skinna's house, she'd made it easy for Hans to get in. But why did he steal the cufflinks, the brooch, the scissors, and the letter opener?

Skinno took off his suit jacket, threw it to Skinna, letting his voice swell like the minister preaching hell from the pulpit. "I know your kind! The kind incapable of taking responsibility. Blame others is your motto. You're nothing but a hopeless, vicious little brute, ready for the reformatory."

Natalie was outraged to hear Hans's saying he'd come because she'd asked him!

Perhaps Hans could think of nothing else in his defense, or he just wanted rid of giant Skinno, who was ready to thrash him. She watched Hans standing still, averting his eyes.

"Our Natalie will have nothing to do with you. She gets everything she needs from us. Go, crawl away like a bug and hide. If I ever see you within a kilometer of us or this house, I'll break every bone in your body, you lout," he shouted. "Leave! Now! Run! Make sure you never return."

Hans gave Natalie a pleading look. "But, Natalie told me," he insisted with a meek voice.

"Not another word. Get out, or I'll pound you into the floor right now." Skinno raised his arm. Hans hurried sideways along the wall and bolted out the front door, that slammed closed behind him. Skinno picked up the jacket Skinna had draped on the back of a chair. Skinna opened her handbag, brought out her compact and powdered her forehead, as she had done at the Franco-Swiss border. As a lady, she must be impeccable at all times!

Edith rang the lunch bell, but Natalie didn't care. As if Skinno had expelled her too, she tore up the stairs to her room. From her window, she saw Hans nonchalantly reach the end of the rose-bordered alley, head down. But once at the gate, he pumped his long legs up and down, his fists began to punch the air fast as he moved out along the grey street. Picking up speed, he galloped away as if a mad dog was about to sink its fangs into him.

Though Skinno had defended her reading, Natalie hated him more than ever. Why did he say, "Our Natalie?" She wasn't theirs. She hated Hans too, for telling lies about her to get out of his troubles. Why did Hans lie? She didn't care that his mother was a cleaning woman! Why had Hans told her that his mother had gone to Lausanne to buy fancy hats? Why did he invent a war hero with medals for a father? Hans had been her friend. What had changed? What had happened to him? He'd taught her to play checkers. "Who taught you?" she'd asked. His father had taught him, a European chess champion, he had claimed.

Hans had shared his cherries with her. Had he stolen the basket or the cherries? Or both? Hans could do complicated arithmetic in his head. That showed he was intelligent. Why did he tell Skinno that she couldn't read? That was dumb! She slammed the window shut and it felt good to make so much noise. She sat on her bed and wondered. Who had told Skinno that Hans was her friend? Who had told him about Hans and his family? Was it the school or someone from the church?

How was she to figure it out all by herself? She could not ask Papa. It would only worry him. Where was Hélène when she needed her? Natalie cried without making a sound, rubbing her tears against her cheeks, wishing someone would come in and hug her tight. Hans had been her friend for such a short while. But no one came. She had lost the only friend near her age in Switzerland.

A grim-faced Natalie dressed early on Monday morning. At school, the boy who sat next to Hans threw his foot in front of Natalie as she passed out test papers. She fell. Test papers flew everywhere. The girls tittered. The boys snickered. The teacher waited for Natalie to get up, trying to ignore her sore elbow. Then the teacher went on helping a girl at the blackboard, taking the hand holding the chalk, asking every few minutes, "Do you understand?"

Why didn't anyone ask her whether she understood what went on? Natalie went next door to choose books to take home, rubbing her sore elbow. One thing was clear. Nobody at school liked her. When the noon bell rang for lunch break, Hans was the first out the door, never looking at her as he led a group of charging boys right past her.

She was glad to see them leave. After the last child walked out and the teacher had gone, Natalie erased the blackboard using wide arcs. She picked up her bag of books, and went by the principal's office, which was empty. Then she saw Hans and three other boys at the school gate, each straddling a bicycle.

When Natalie tried to walk past them, Hans shouted, "Going back to France, refugee?"

Stung, she returned indoors. After a few minutes, she tried again. But the boys on their bikes formed a barricade in front of her and chanted, "We don't want her, send the refugee packing."

Natalie wanted nothing more than to dash across the street, but any of the boys could catch her. Hans edged forward on his bike. Did he borrow it? He'd told her he didn't want a bike because he was waiting for a motorcycle from his father. For once, she was sorry to admit, Skinno had been right. Hans told lies.

She retreated inside the school for a bit, then started out again, hoping the boys had gone home for lunch. But they came pedaling toward her on the now empty street, screaming, "re-fu-gee, re-fu-gee!"

A mean, terrible word. So ugly! Natalie plugged her ears with her fingers. She went back to sit on the outer steps of the school and wait, however long she must, for the janitor to arrive.

After a while, she noticed someone advancing up the hill toward her. As the woman came closer, Natalie recognized the green hat and matching leather purse. Skinna, returning from the hairdresser! Natalie didn't get up. Skinna scowled when she found her on the steps. "Natalie! Why aren't you home, washing your hands for lunch?" Skinna scolded. "Get up!"

As if Skinna was half-deaf, Natalie sat still and shouted, "The boys won't let me leave!"

"What boys? There's no one about." Skinna adjusted her pillbox hat with its veil.

"Look around the corner, if you don't believe me," Natalie spat out. "They're hiding with their bikes."

"Why do you associate with these hooligans, instead of playing with nice girls? I thought you'd learned your lesson yesterday! Your uncle will be quite angry."

"If it's someone's fault, it's not mine," Natalie shouted, wishing she had the courage to say it was all Skinna's fault for agreeing to send her to remedial classes she didn't need. "I have nothing to do with the boys, but they won't let me pass."

Skinna kept shaking her head from side to side. "Does it have to do with that boy, Hans?"

"He pedaled away when he saw you," said Natalie. "The other three hooligans are his friends. Now I guess they'll let me pass," she said. She was glad to call them hooligans, she liked saying that word. Getting up, dusting off her clothes, she picked up her book bag and walked onto the street without waiting for Skinna, who couldn't walk as fast on her high heels. No one stopped them at the crossroad or further along the way.

Skinno came in late for lunch. During the meal, he was frowning and severe. He spoke of nothing but the unfairness of diminishing funds for his lab. Skinna nodded several times, uttering bland remarks and making little balls from the soft part of her bread roll, lining them between her wine glass and her plate. She made no mention of boys harassing Natalie.

Hans did not return to school the next day, or the day after that, or the following week. Would Hans ever learn to read? How could reading hurt his eyes? Natalie couldn't help wondering whether he was again entering someone's home, taking what he could stuff into his pockets.

But she also thought that he might be home, very sorry, promising himself never to do such a thing again. People could change. Captain Nemo, in *Twenty Thousand Leagues Under the Sea*, had surely changed by the end of the story.

She missed Hans. She didn't miss the Hans that Skinno had described. She missed her friend, the only person her age to do fun things with, not the boy who couldn't read and didn't care to learn—the cheat, the thief, the liar.

Chapter 27

To Escape

In August, the radio said that there were important developments in Italy. What did it mean? Skinno was arriving back home in five days, and she was counting down the days. Skinno would be back in five, then four, and then, in another three days. Skinna was on the phone, checking and rechecking lists of families willing to take in new refugee children. Natalie sneakily spent more time with Papa.

Natalie was leaning against the back wall of the house near one of the small windows of the basement, reading *Heidi*. Pierre was busy adding a shelf down there. Edith waited, ready to load it with jars of black cherry jam she'd made the day before.

"Monsieur is very impatient with Natalie, did you notice?" Edith asked Pierre.

"Don't you dare say anything, Edith, or we'd both get into trouble," Pierre replied, "I don't think Madame is any better, if you want know," he said. "Poor little one, so pretty and bright, don't you agree? What a shame she has such cold-hearted relatives. Now, pick up both of your baskets, Edith, or you'll hunt for them in the morning," he said, as they both left the basement full of provisions.

Natalie knew, from talk in the kitchen, that Skinna was going to Lausanne after lunch the next day, to meet Skinno. He was coming from Paris, accompanying a train full of sick children. Skinna had taken her once to meet the children's train when Edith had a day off and couldn't keep an eye on her.

While Skinna made her calls, Natalie sat in her room trying to draw like Papa, or at least like Hélène. First, for Maman, she drew Tante Pauline's house, then Pierre, and canoes with oars on a beach. When she had four drawings, she folded them. Tomorrow she would ask Papa for an envelope. Oncle Marc would think they were Papa's letters, and he would take them to France in his briefcase on his way back.

Natalie's spying window on the balcony was shut since the sky was crowded with rain clouds. So she hid behind the tapestry that hung in front of the suitcase closet of Papa's anteroom.

Through the door to Papa's room, Natalie heard Skinna say, "From now on, with the Allies in Sicily, everything will improve in Europe, and for you as well. We'll call Schwartz in Bern."

Sicily was a part of Italy. How could the Allies be there? Natalie wondered. Everybody hoped for an invasion by the Allies, but where could they land? She didn't have time to figure it out because Papa spoke to Skinna.

He replied crossly, "Out of the question."

Natalie heard him trying to stop his strangled cough. He added, "I refuse to see another specialist. As for that ass, Perelman, I'd rather climb the Matterhorn than see his face again."

Skinna put one of her favorite Brahms records on the turntable. Splendid chords swirled over Natalie. She found herself in a musical cocoon.

The door opened. A panel of light slid with Brahms ripples between the door and the tapestry. Natalie glimpsed

Skinna as she left Papa's room wearing a fancy blue hat with a short veil. The hat wobbled when Skinna closed the door. In front of the house, Pierre would already be holding the car door open for Madame. He had to obey Skinna, but Natalie knew that Pierre enjoyed helping Papa, and would do anything for him.

Papa said, "Come in!"

Natalie stepped out from behind the tapestry and walked into his room. "Can you really climb the Matterhorn?"

"You scalawag, listening behind the door!" On the white bedcover, Papa's long-fingered hands were yellow. "I heard you sneak in behind Tante Pauline," he said.

Boldly, she said, "Pierre said he would. I mean, drive us away to wherever you choose."

Papa stiffened. "Did they enroll you as well in their doctor rigmarole?"

"You don't understand, Papa. All you have to do is come along. Pierre said he would drive us anywhere when you want to go. He will. He said so, I asked him yesterday. We can go to the bridge on the river." She longed for him to feel her urgency.

"The bridge? Ah, you mean our symbolic bridge." Coughing shook him. He spat into his metal-lidded cup.

She wasn't sure what symbolic meant, but it sounded positive—bright and secret.

"So many decisions!" Papa sighed, passing his hand over his forehead. "I wouldn't last ten minutes in my pajamas."

"No. You'd be very cold outside. First, I'll help you dress. You can put your suit on over your pajamas and wear your wool socks. I know where they are."

"And our luggage?" Papa asked.

"I can carry the rucksack. I've been practicing. I can

carry a suitcase too, if it's not too heavy. You can lean on my shoulder. I won't walk fast, I promise."

"What if there is a storm?"

Natalie was astonished, "Are you afraid of thunder, Papa?"

"Aren't you afraid of it, just a little?" he asked.

"No. It's beautiful. But I don't like cold water—to wade in, I mean."

Papa said very softly, "We might get lost in the mountains."

"I have the map you made and my compass."

"What about the fox?"

Natalie liked the fox. "He doesn't bite people."

"You're not afraid of animals in the wild?"

"People are more—are scarier than foxes," she said, seeing Oncle Marc in her mind.

Papa looked at her strangely. "Tell me, are you seriously planning to run away?"

"It's not running away if I am with you!" she cried.

In his softest voice, Papa said, "Don't worry, *Petites Nattes*, we'll cross plenty of bridges soon. Very soon, it'll be time to go home."

He waved her out of his room.

She wished him a good night and climbed to her room. Even though Papa was cross, he said they would soon go home. Natalie reminded herself that this was good news. As long as she had Papa, she was safe. She hummed "A la Claire Fontaine" to herself as she went to bed. Yes, she was sure they were going home because Papa had said so. Did the Skinnies know? She sat up in bed. It was probably a secret. She slid down inside the covers and curled up under the eiderdown.

Papa had a passport, but she didn't. Would the customs

people, or the Germans, throw her into prison when they found out? She wasn't twelve yet. She pulled the bed sheet around her neck. At home, there was a war. It started when she was only eight, in 1939, and now it was 1943. Soon, on August twenty-six, she would be twelve years old.

Would she feel very different? Would she have her twelfth birthday in Montreux with Skinna? Her pillow felt hard under her head. She turned over onto her stomach. No. She would have her birthday in France with her whole family. A French newspaper that Skinno had left in the sitting room said that families in France were entitled to one egg per week. One egg to share? One egg wouldn't be enough to make a big birthday cake. What about flour? When Edith made a cake, she took flour and eggs and sugar.

If Maman made a cake for her birthday, she would give her slice to Papa. What about the war? People died in wars. She didn't want anybody to die. Especially not Papa. Natalie drifted into sleep among her worries.

In the morning, Skinno found Natalie in the sitting room. "*Mon Dieu*, that girl is always underfoot. Find something to do, or go outside," he grumbled. As though she were a dog.

She went upstairs and brought down her letter to Hélène. She had included the drawings for Maman, and hoped Skinno would put it in his briefcase and mail it on his next trip. When she gave it to Skinno, he said, "Someone tell her there is no mail to France from Switzerland."

Natalie felt more afraid than hurt. Would she ever be able to send something to Maman?

That night, at barely seven o'clock, Skinno asked, "Isn't it time the child was in bed?"

Natalie knew that Skinno hated her. She hated him back. She was glad she'd opened his lab cages so that his mice and rabbits had run away. She had wanted to help them escape. She had apologized, because he forced her, but she was not sorry.

After supper, Natalie asked Skinna, "Why does papa no longer sit on the balcony?"

"It's getting too cold now to sit outside," said Skinna.

Natalie had spent the whole summer in Montreux, where Papa was not getting any better. "Why does the doctor come almost every day?"

"Francis likes to chat with him." Skinna twirled gold bracelets over her silk sleeves.

"That's not true! You make me go away when he opens his bag."

Skinna said, "Papa's getting better, but he still has a long way to go. Don't tire him with silly chit-chat."

Grown-ups didn't always make sense. Natalie knew it was better not to ask for explanations. When she did, she only made people angry.

Before lunch on Sunday, she asked Papa, "When are you going to get up again?"

He said, "Soon, *Petites Nattes,* very soon."

"Promise to get up for my birthday, Papa. Please, Papa?"

"Let me see. August twenty-six is three weeks from Friday. Don't worry. I'll be up. Up and dressed for your birthday." Papa opened his picture calendar. Natalie counted. She had to wait only twenty-four more days to be twelve years old, almost grown-up.

Chapter 28

Telling Pierre

Natalie was happy thinking about Papa getting up for her birthday. Even at school, she was once again to help the teacher stack books that had been returned to the library. In a week, she'd be twelve, she thought on her way back home for lunch. She stepped into Skinna's home, imagining Papa beside her, about to blow out her birthday candles with her. But no one was downstairs. From the upstairs landing, Skinna called down to her, "Wait down-stairs in the entryway."

She waited till she ached all over, twisting on the bench by the umbrella stand. She sensed a presence on the upstairs landing, so huge it darkened the stairwell. Without looking up, she knew it was Skinno. If only he were sick instead of Papa! In her mind, she saw Skinno in a narrow bed with Skinna crying beside him. Papa was phoning from far away, telling them he was on a trip with Natalie. Papa also told Oncle Marc that he could no longer work in the lab because his sickness would kill the caged animals.

Natalie's daydream dissolved when someone came running down the stairs. It was Edith, with a balled-up handkerchief under her nose. On her way to the kitchen, she passed in front of Natalie without seeing her. Natalie had never seen Edith cry. Maids cried when the woman of the house said mean things to them. Skinna must have said very mean things. She could hear Skinno upstairs, talking to people who were walking overhead. "*Mon Dieu*, all those wine bottles! Poor fellow," Skinno said.

He left the stairwell before Natalie could say, "I don't like when you say, 'Poor fellow'." Papa was sick, he wasn't poor.

Natalie wondered what it meant. What kind of bottles? Were they medicine bottles, or something else? Were they the whatnots Pierre had brought in?

Natalie continued to sit in the hall, concerned about the strange events and whether anyone was going to bring out her afternoon lunch. It usually consisted of a soft buttered roll into which she inserted a narrow Lindt chocolate bar. On Sundays she drank a glass of apple juice with an ice cube in it. Ice was bad for children. They could die from swallowing ice, Edith had told her.

Natalie was hungry and bored in the house that smelled of wax and polish. She looked out the back into the garden to see that pink and orange gladiolas jutted above white cosmos and marigold borders. The sky was blue. She ran down the steps and up again, counting, to see how often she ended on a lucky number, with or without crossing her fingers. The fruit and vegetable crates delivered each Tuesday after lunch lined the steps. She plucked a dappled pink and red apple from the closest box and pushed it into her pocket.

Insects buzzed in the sun. She tried not to make the pebbles crunch. Without turning around, Natalie saw the back of the house in her mind, its balconies around the second and third floor with cutout decorations in a heart pattern repeated on each shutter.

She walked along the road to St. Benoît village. At the slope, she stared at a statue of Christ on the cross. His sadness poured into her so that when she bit into the apple, her mouth filled with bitter, sour juice. She spat out the chunk of fruit and dumped the apple back into her pocket.

Passing a patch of nettles she decided to pick a few. She knew how to keep from being stung. She chose long ones, not too hairy, to carry on her shoulder. Nettles were useless. Natalie lifted the stems and let the bunch fall behind her without looking. Across the path, a red slug made silver tracks. They nauseated her. She never wanted to see a slug again.

There was a pebble under her big toe. She curled her toes under and sat down on the sidewalk to shake out her sandal. It must be time to go back. No, she thought. She wasn't going yet. "I want to see Pierre," she said to no one, confused by questions and feelings swirling inside her. She turned around.

She went to see Pierre almost every day. He gave her mints or caramels and called her "little one." It felt good, but she worried in case she was seen talking with him. It was against the rules because he was a servant.

She turned around and walked back. Nearing the house she had a feeling that something terrible had happened. What? It didn't seem possible that Papa had died. Everybody was upstairs. Nobody spoke to her. Today she would call the gardener "Monsieur," rather than Pierre, to sound more grown-up.

Pierre was in the garden, tending gladiolas in the sun and bluebells in the shade, his face red from bending down. He smiled when he saw coming, smiling as she made her way through the tomato vines, impatiens, dahlias, and beside the little islands set aside for thyme, chervil, and tarragon. He stood up with ease, his large body comfortable in his overalls. Natalie liked his checkered shirts. She wished he'd worn one today. He kissed her cheek as usual.

"Monsieur Pierre," she said, embarrassed by her solemnity, wanting to tell him but also needing to ask, "Do you think something bad has happened?"

Pierre hesitated. She added, "I waited a long time in the kitchen, but Edith didn't come. She stayed upstairs."

Had Papa died? No, he couldn't have. Papa had spoken with her yesterday. He'd even waved to her. People didn't die if they could wave. She looked up at Pierre, knowing Papa had died, as if she'd expected it all along. She felt her understanding grow so large that she felt old, too old for her body, not quite twelve. Pierre cried large tears, effortlessly, so many of them. Natalie had never seen a man cry.

"*Jésus-Marie*! We knew it was coming, but we are not ready," said Pierre, as he gathered her up in his arms. She smelled the good smell of freshly turned earth on his loose blue shirt. He kissed her cheek, gently, as if she would break. She didn't know how to return his kindness, or console him, as he went on crying while she had no tears.

Feeling in his overall pocket, after blowing his nose in his handkerchief, Pierre said, "I nearly forgot. Look what I set aside for you." He handed her a perfect peach.

She forgot to be embarrassed. Pierre treated her like a grown-up, although she wasn't sure she'd ever be one, because it took so very long. Pierre was good, all good, like Papa. She thanked him, her present in her hand. She said, "I must go now," remembering her manners.

Chapter 29

A Peach

It was the best peach of the season—that was certain—the kind picked for the Lalique basket when guests came to dinner. Natalie held it firmly in her hands, looking at it intensely. She must concentrate on the peach. That was what mattered. Nothing else. The peach. She needed someone to show it to, to admire it, to share it. Who could it be? Only vaguely did she think of Maman, Hélène and Lilla in France where there was a war. Lise and Michelle from summer school had gone to the fair. The beekeeper who made funny faces to make her laugh? He had his own peaches. Pierre? It couldn't be Pierre. He had given the peach to her.

Who, then, would smile and take the peach in a hollow palm, praise it and carefully bite into the sun-warmed juiciness? Nobody.

She ran around Skinna's house. Shutters, windows, doors, were all shut. The house was horrible. Natalie returned to the front, quaking like the lake shaking fists during storms. The geraniums she'd helped to plant were bleeding monsters. Ugly, everything was ugly. She didn't want to think about the people hiding from her inside the house.

She stood on the front path, swung her arm back and forth two or three times, then, aiming at the wall, she threw the perfect peach onto the facade so hard, she thought she would lose her balance, while she told herself, with intense despair mixed with satisfaction, "I'm wicked, very wicked."

Chapter 30

Funeral

On the steps of the church, at Papa's funeral five days later, Natalie ran to the black-robed minister and clung to him. "*Dites-leur,* Monsieur. Please, tell them to wait for Maman. She wants to come. Please, make them wait."

The minister put a hand on her shoulder. "Your mother can't come, child. She's not allowed."

The chapel was cold. Only seven people had come. Skinna sat, all in black, at the front, weeping under her black veil next to Skinno, both sitting away from the other people. No one told Natalie where to sit. She sat by herself, three rows behind them, crushing her hands against each other or hugging herself.

Afterwards, at home, the Skinnies talked behind closed doors. When Skinna came out, she was sobbing as if her own Papa had died. Oncle Marc helped her to their room. Then he came back downstairs, mumbling about a hysterical woman on one hand and a crazy child on the other.

Natalie ate a cold dinner in the kitchen with a red-eyed Edith staring at her. Edith took a tray up to the Skinnies for their dinner. The next day Natalie was not allowed to see Pierre, because it wasn't proper. When she tried to get into Papa's room, she found the door locked and the French windows on the balcony shuttered.

In the living room, some paintings had been removed to make room for one of Papa's lake landscapes. The photo of Papa clowning with Skinno in front of the Villa Florence was still on the table. They both had plenty of hair, and their faces had no wrinkles. Their arms were around each other's waists. They were laughing, each with a foot up in the air in front of them.

Natalie wanted to cut Skinno out of the photo, and slice his mean face into a trillion snippets, but Skinna would find out.

"Papa made a drawing of a feather for my birthday," Natalie lied. Her birthday was coming on Saturday, and she wanted something special from Papa. "I'm going to take it home."

"You can't take home that thing full of germs," Skinna said. She was still wearing her black clothes and stood looking at the wall where she'd hung Papa's drawing of lilies of the valley.

"Papa's things are not yours," Natalie blurted out.

Skinna let the outburst pass. "We asked the Red Cross to contact your mother."

"You should have told her first!" Natalie exploded.

"What difference could that make?" Skinno said. "Your mother isn't allowed out of France."

"What's to happen?" Natalie asked, crossing her arms by overlapping the sides of her cardigan. She didn't want to stay in Montreux, but if she went back to France without a passport the Germans would kill her, because she was a Jew.

"I see you'd rather stay here," Skinno said, mistaking her shivers for a desire to stay in Switzerland. "However, your aunt's sister broke her arm. She needs your aunt Pauline's help. We had agreed to take you for one or two months at most. And though it's utter madness, your mother told the Red Cross she wants you back at home."

At the thought of home, Natalie trembled from fear and anticipation, and the terrible knowledge that Papa wouldn't be coming home with her.

Chapter 31

Going Home

After breakfast the next day, the Skinnies faced each other in the sitting room when Natalie walked in, surprised by their silence.

"Is the war over?" she asked.

"The war's far from over, but you are going home all the same," said Skinna. "Tomorrow, your uncle will buy your return ticket. Go and ask Edith to make a label for your rucksack."

"I can make my own label. I know how. Can I have a box to take Papa's drawings? Please," she added, giddy at the thought of going home so soon, though not at all the way she had hoped. "A flat box, not too big."

"Ah, the drawings." Skinna stood up. "The drawings had to be burned, along with your father's books, his clothes and everything else," Skinna declared. "Remember when I told you not to touch Papa? Tuberculosis spreads to other people. It would not be safe to keep his belongings." She shook her gray shawl and draped it around her before sitting down.

Natalie couldn't believe what horrid Skinna was telling her. She asked, "Why did you lock the doors to Papa's room?"

"That room needed to be fumigated to kill the germs."

Natalie's chest tightened. "Why do you keep Papa's landscapes?"

"Oh, those aren't recent," Skinna said, sounding vague.

Something was wrong with Skinna's explanation. Natalie couldn't think what.

Would Skinna burn her rucksack, her compass, and the pocketknife Papa had given her, because of the tuberculosis in his room?

She could not believe that she would never see Papa again, still she knew the gifts were all she had left of him. She hid them between the bedsprings and the mattress on her bed, checking often, imagining that Skinno and Skinna were mistaken, that Papa would soon return. Maybe he'd only been taken to another hospital with new medicine for a few days, and his medical papers had been exchanged by mistake with another patient's.

A week after Papa's funeral, making sure Skinna wasn't looking, Natalie passed the sitting room table and snatched a box of matches. Then when Skinna went to answer the telephone, she crept up to the photo table and took a small candle sitting at the back, and put the short silver candlestick quietly into a drawer. Nobody would miss it. She ran to her room with the candle stub, listening through the closed door. All was quiet. She struck the match, protecting the flame with her hand, as Papa used to do when he lit cigarettes at home. She brought the flame to the wick. It gave a pale glow.

The door burst open. Skinno strode in. "Give those back."

"It's my birthday," Natalie protested. She was twelve now.

"I don't believe you."

Natalie cried, "It's true! My birthday is on the twenty-sixth." Papa had promised to be up. At the thought, burning tears gushed out. "Ask Grand-Maman," she said between sobs, searching for her handkerchief. "She knows everybody's birthday. Mine's a month before Papa's."

Skinno took the candle and left.

On Thursday after breakfast, Skinna, all in black, told Pierre to drive her and Natalie to town. There she bought Natalie a pair of plain brown shoes with laces, a pot of honey, two chocolate bars and a packet of Lekerli cookies.

"In Switzerland we have plenty of food, but in France there's a war," Skinna said as if Natalie knew nothing about it. "The day after tomorrow you are going home." They walked back to the car. Natalie slowed down to look at the children's shop window were she'd seen a coat with gold buttons like those on Papa's uniform. Skinna slowed down too. "We can't send you home in something so unsuitable."

It would be useless to argue with stupid Skinna.

Back at the villa, nobody said anything about her birthday. Skinna went upstairs.

Skinno said, "Do you understand how fortunate you've been all summer? Eating your fill of breads and cakes, butter, meat and cheese, gobbling cherries and chocolate, getting a full wardrobe? Don't you have anything to say?" He waited. "Your aunt is so shocked by your ingratitude that she's taken to her bed." He waited.

"My Papa died!" Natalie wanted to scream. But the words stuck in her throat like fish bones.

When Skinna came down for supper in her orange silk robe, Natalie asked, "Is Maman home? With Hélène and Lilla? Does she know I'm coming?"

"She knows."

"How? You never let me write."

"Letters can't cross the border. But we have contacts in France through the Red Cross. They told your mother."

Without her make-up, Skinna looked old. "It's time for

you to say something important to us." The more she insisted that Natalie say "thank you," the less she wanted to say it. She looked at the hem of the drapes. There was something Natalie wanted to say.

"Oncle Marc never took my drawings to France," Natalie said when she saw Skinno come and stand behind Skinna.

"If he said he would, he certainly did," Skinna said.

"No, he didn't," Natalie exploded. "He threw my drawings into the rubbish bin." She glared at Skinna. "I know why he didn't take them," she said, forcing herself to copy her aunt's reasonable tone.

Skinno stepped out from behind Skinna's chair.

"And why is that?" Skinna asked, raising an eyebrow.

"Because he's like Grand-Pere," said Natalie.

With both hands in front of her, Skinna examined her unpolished nails. "And according to you, how is Marc like Grand-Pere?"

"They hate Jews, that's how," Natalie concluded, crossing her arms over her chest.

"Where did you hear such nonsense? Did you expect your uncle to endanger himself by contacting your mother?"

"He could have put my drawings in an envelope with a stamp on it when he went back to France," Natalie raged. Skinna was silent. Natalie added, "I only came with you to see Papa."

Skinna didn't move, but Skinno strode toward Natalie. Once in front of her, he let the back of his hand fly to the side of her face.

Natalie's hand rose to the burning spot. "When Maman slaps me," she said, doing her best to keep her voice steady, "I still love her."

Skinno spoke as if talking to himself. "I never wanted

this responsibility and this is why. You may look like your father, but you are nothing like him, except for his weakness. Go to your room and stay there!" He returned to the piano and sat in front of his Debussy Etudes.

"I will!" Natalie cried. "You are wicked! I don't want to see you ever again." She slammed the door behind her and ran up the stairs. Soon, she'd be rid of the nasty Skinnies, who understood nothing. She was glad they didn't have children. It served them right. They were too mean to have them, and would only make them unhappy.

Chapter 32

Last Dinner in Switzerland

Instead of eating in the kitchen, Natalie had to eat her last dinner in Montreux in the dining room with the Skinnies, so that she couldn't see Pierre. There were the usual silver forks, knives and dessert spoons on the tablecloth, but they were no longer interesting. No one spoke to her. She looked down into her plate as Edith served her roasted potatoes, fish in cream sauce and tiny green beans. The Skinnies made small talk together.

With a rough movement, Skinno knocked his glass of red wine into the salt cruet, which fell sideways onto the tablecloth. The wine inched around the dish of green beans.

Laughter erupted from Natalie's mouth before she knew it. Skinna shuddered. Skinno's face reddened. He slapped his napkin over the burgundy stain. Natalie kept laughing a sad, gurgling, choking laughter, as if Hélène sat across from her. The seated grown-ups looked at each other. Natalie caught their horrified expression, which she knew meant "the worst child we've ever seen."

Natalie closed her mouth. Her laughter rose and hovered like a startled hummingbird out of one of Papa's books, whirling close to mean Skinno and silly Skinna's ears and their eyes, asking to be let in. When they turned away, the tiny bird rose higher and higher and dissolved into the crystals of the chandelier. It was as if she hadn't laughed at all.

With dinner over Natalie wanted to escape, but Skinna told her to follow her. She opened her bureau drawer and brought out two coloring books, the kind a five-year-old would like, and handed Natalie an unwrapped box of colored pencils. "For your birthday," said Skinna.

Natalie had to say "thank you" even though the presents weren't any good. She ran upstairs to throw the coloring books into the wastebasket. She kept the pencils for Hélène.

In France, only rich girls like Georgette had colored pencils.

Natalie quietly tiptoed downstairs to find Edith. Yet once in the kitchen, she didn't know what to say to Edith, who was scraping leftovers off the dinner plates. "Do you see Pierre sometimes?" Natalie asked.

"I see him plenty, seeing that he's my husband," she said without turning around.

Natalie was dumbstruck. It hadn't occurred to her that Edith could be somebody's wife.

"Tell him—say—say goodbye for me. Goodbye, Edith." Natalie wished she could tell Edith how much she liked Pierre, and that she liked her too. Finding the right words was too hard. Edith was already sniffling over the sink, pulling a handkerchief from her sleeve. Natalie ran out.

She was still eleven. She drew herself up to stand tall. Tomorrow, on her twelfth birthday, she was going back to France by herself. She thought of Grand-Papa, Maman's father, who had let her play with his jade Buddha and made her feel special for a little while. She'd been four years old then and believed there might be many more such moments, but her hopes were dashed when, a few months later, Grand-

Papa had died suddenly. Now she realized that Maman had her Papa much longer than she had had her clever Papa. Natalie had cried herself to sleep at night when no one understood why she was so unhappy. She had learned why some people said that life was unfair. Yes. It was unfair that Grand-Pere had died. Natalie felt things were worse for her, but now she had no tears.

Chapter 33

To the Train Station

On Thursday, the day she was leaving, Natalie was told to wear two outfits on top of each other again—as she had done over four months ago to cross the border between France and Switzerland. She had to make room in her rucksack for socks, a nightie, shorts, a toilet bag with a tube of toothpaste, and her cardigan, as well as cookies and a jar of honey. Edith had made her a sandwich, wrapped in wax paper. The grey coat she was given was secondhand. Skinna had said a used coat was safer going through customs, but Natalie knew it was because the Skinnies hated her.

The Skinnos didn't practice loving everybody; they were not like Papa. She was tempted to take the Heidi book home with her, but wasn't sure she should. She left it under her pillow. She didn't have to kiss Skinna good bye, because Skinna took medicine at night since Papa had died and was still asleep when it was time for Natalie to leave. Pierre was nowhere to be seen.

It was Skinno who drove Natalie to the Montreux station and put her on the train. No one sat in her compartment. He placed her rucksack and small bag on the shelf above her head, and told her to sit by the window. From inside the pocket of his overcoat Skinno pulled a thick envelope with three red wax stamps and a loop of strings extending from the top edge. He handed it to Natalie and watched as she put the loop over her head so it hung around her neck. "Keep it on you at all times, do you understand?" he instructed. Natalie nodded. "You must show it only at the border when asked for your passport."

He then told her to ask for help to lower her bag and rucksack when she changed trains on the French side of the border. He looked at her for a moment without expression. She nodded again, thinking he wanted her agreement. Then he said, "I'd better be going then." Natalie felt confused. She was the one who was leaving.

He held his hand toward hers and they shook hands with their fingers barely touching. Skinno walked out of the compartment onto the platform and left her sitting at the window.

Natalie didn't think he'd wave, but just in case she clutched the coat on her lap and leaned forward as she watched him walk farther and farther away, crossing paths with the conductor who hurried past her window toward the engine, waving a red flag. From the soles of her feet to the base of her neck, Natalie felt the tremor of the electric train taking off, returning her to the border with France.

Chapter 34

In France Again

In Le Vésinet armed Germans in grey-green uniforms were everywhere—in shops, around the train station, in the streets, in the market, around the police station, and pushing children on their way home off the sidewalks. The uniform helmets covered their ears and hid their eyebrows, so they looked like insects inside their hard shell. People called the soldiers *doryphores,* potato beetles, because the German army took all the potatoes to feed their men.

Maman was the same. Natalie didn't hug her because Maman didn't like emotional demonstrations.

She'd been gone months. The garden looked smaller. Everything was smaller and dusty or broken. The lawn was dug up and planted with potatoes, the way poor people did. Natalie was to do the watering. No flowers had been planted. Everything looked old and worn, especially the house. The furniture, the walls, and the rug on the stairs looked shabby. Natalie was surprised not to have noticed it before. She looked for Lilla, but her little sister was in bed with a fever. Hearing the commotion downstairs as Natalie arrived, Lilla came down from her room in her double pajamas, to be warm. She had grown taller and thinner.

"Her feet are too big for her shoes," Maman said.

Hélène was the same. Meaning more grown, unchanged, not ill. After bedtime, Natalie crept into her sister's room. All she could see in the dark was a white pillowcase with Hélène's head on it as she spoke. "Lilla went to Mademoiselle Leblanc. I went to Grand-Papa and Grand-Maman. And you?"

Natalie's eyes adjusted to the dark as she sat on the edge of the bed. "I went to the Skinnies in Montreux."

Hélène blinked, "Who?"

"I thought I had told you." Natalie explained, "Oncle Marc looks so perfect, but he's nothing like Papa. And Tante Pauline, I don't like her. I had to call her Maman until Switzerland. She gave me the Heidi book, but that's the only good thing she did. I call them the Skinnies. He's Skinno, and she's Skinna, because they are so—skinny."

Hélène laughed. "The Skinnies! Super names, but everybody is skinny here, you see."

Natalie sighed. She didn't want to let go of these perfect new names and return to calling them Oncle Marc, and Tante Pauline.

"Just call them Marc and Pauline," said Hélène. "Don't use Oncle or Tante."

Natalie was mildly comforted.

Hélène frowned. "Still, it was not fair! You went to Switzerland when I should have gone! Maman had promised."

Natalie murmured, "I didn't choose to go to the Skinnies."

Hélène straightened up so fast that Natalie thought they were about to fight, but instead, they hugged. They pretended to have been separated only a week or two. After all, sisters were meant to live together, Hélène said. Telling most of what had happened far away would make them feel awkward. Natalie crept back into her room and her cold bed.

A few times, Hélène asked, "What did Papa say to you?

What did you talk about?"

Natalie couldn't think of their conversations or even the sound of his voice. "I don't remember," she admitted. But at night, she dreamed of Papa. In her dreams, they had wonderful talks.

Maman never asked about Papa, Marc, Pauline, or how Natalie had crossed into Switzerland.

A few weeks later, when the October rain blew around the house, Maman stayed downstairs helping Lilla with her spelling homework. Natalie was upstairs in her room with Hélène, the two sitting side by side assembling a wildflower puzzle that took a long time. In a low voice, Hélène asked about Papa's death. At first, Natalie found nothing to say. Taking her time, she asked, "Do you mean the funeral?" She found a red puzzle piece to complete a poppy.

Hélène didn't look at her. She asked, "Were you with him when he died?"

"I was at summer school," Natalie said, pretending to scan the remaining puzzle pieces. "The doctor came almost every day, but no one told me that Papa was—" she trailed off, turning a puzzle piece in her hand. "I didn't know until I had to try on a brown skirt from the Red Cross that Edith hemmed up for me."

"To attend the funeral?" asked Hélène.

"To wear with a white blouse," Natalie hurried on. "The minister said Maman wasn't allowed into Switzerland. There were only seven people in the chapel. The minister and the doctor went to the cemetery in front of Pauline and Marc. I walked behind them. Edith and Pierre came too."

The floor creaked in the passage behind them. They turned around to the doorway, and saw Maman, her back to them, walking silently away. They resumed assembling the puzzle, neither of them talking.

Did Maman know she was wicked because of what she had done in Skinno's lab?

It took Natalie several days to again get used to life in war-torn France—scarcity of food, sandbags piled high around the cathedral, boarded-up spaces where stained-glass windows used to glow, uncollected trash on sidewalks, and untrimmed shrubs. She saw only glimpses of public parks full of weeds from the street as she passed by with Maman, who wasn't allowed in public places. Neither was she allowed in cinemas, theaters, or even to use a public telephone in a booth on the street or in a café or restaurant. Natalie again saw walls everywhere in need of paint, ugly propaganda posters, shop windows filled with empty tin cans, and portraits of Marshall Pétain plastered in every classroom, shop, post office, and public hall.

She'd forgotten how people had to wait in long lines, sometimes for hours, outside the grocer's, the dairy, the baker's, the hardware or the pharmacy. Now lines of people stood waiting in the rain and the snow, even in the heat, even when the wind was strong enough to sweep them away. Back at home were the familiar bread bags, hanging on the back of each one's chair, holding their daily slice of bitter bread.

After school one afternoon, they went with Maman to buy stamps at the post office.

The baker's wife, ahead of them in line, said, "That's the way it is." The post office clerk said the same thing. Hélène said that the clerk was a widow.

Natalie asked, "What does that mean?"

"That's when you're so untidy, you lose your husband," Hélène answered.

They had the giggles so badly that tears ran down their cheeks. Maman sent them outside.

"Oh, those terrible years of adolescence!" she said. Later at home, they couldn't remember what had been so funny.

Because the girls talked too often about food, Maman made a rule that no one must speak of it between meals.

Sometimes Maman forgot. She told her girls about lavish nine-course dinners her parents used to offer visiting ambassadors and painters, newly engaged friends, and wedding guests. She described suppers after the theater or the opera with pheasant, sturgeon, or daintily served fresh salmon with curried mayonnaise, accompanied by capers inside carved lemons. She mentioned her big brother Jacob and her little sister Miriam, who was mischievous. Natalie thought Maman must wonder where they were, and didn't understand why she'd never met them. Would she ever?

Fascinated, Natalie and her sisters imagined feasts with quail and caviar, eggs with truffle slices, even though they'd never tasted them. They could see fancy chocolate and praline pastries with wild strawberries on silver trays about to materialize on the yellow, cracked oilcloth of their dining table.

Before calling the girls in to set the kitchen table for dinner, Maman saved the water left after boiling turnips and cabbages for her breakfast, because there was neither coffee nor tea for sale. Maman said that it was good for her. She had tried to make coffee with what the grocer sold, which was roasted barley with much chicory. It didn't smell of coffee, and Maman found it too bitter.

Chapter 35

A Composition

Natalie attended high school now. One Monday in November, Mademoiselle Leblanc, Natalie's French teacher, wrote the subject of the weekly composition on the blackboard.

Natalie wriggled and squirmed with pleasurable anticipation. Soon all was quiet in the classroom. Now and then, Mademoiselle stalked like a policeman between rows of bent heads to snatch up any notes bearing questions that should come rolling by a friend's shoe or under a desk, accidentally of course.

Dipping her pen in the inkwell on her desk, Natalie wrote her full name on the top left of the page. In the right corner, she added the date: Tuesday, November 16, 1943. Then came the title: "How We Spend a Happy Evening."

She wrote fast, on both sides of the rough sheets because paper was in short supply. Natalie read her essay over, making small changes. Then cocking her head, she copied her masterpiece onto the lined paper. She especially enjoyed a big brother she'd invented, brave and kind, and determined. There wasn't a single smear of ink on her page.

In high spirits after handing in her work, Natalie found it hard to sit still until recess. Two seats away, her friend Georgette sulked, then raised her head with a gesture that Natalie read as an appeal. With a discreet flourish, Natalie slipped Georgette one sheet of her own two-page draft. In composition, she was better than Georgette. But Georgette wore new clothes, not hand-me-downs that didn't fit. She didn't wear wood-soled shoes, like Natalie, because her parents bought her leather ones on the black market, and she wore a silver wristwatch.

When the bell rang in the afternoon, Natalie hung her regulation pink overblouse in the cloakroom. Mademoiselle Leblanc confronted her at the door.

"Pleased with your composition, Natalie?"

"Oh, yes. It was fun, Mademoiselle."

"Fun," Mademoiselle repeated, which prompted Natalie to watch her face. "Tell your mother I need to talk to her, will you?"

"Yes, Mademoiselle."

No, she wouldn't. Natalie protested in silence as she walked away. Other girls chatted in class too. Why should she be singled out? Anyway, Mademoiselle had not handed her a written note. She felt unhappy because not telling Maman was a bit like lying.

Natalie started for the playground. She thought about an afternoon before Easter when Maman had been asked come to school, before Natalie had gone to Switzerland. Mademoiselle Leblanc had read Maman a report that still rang painfully in Natalie's mind. "Vivacious child who doesn't apply herself. Lacks perseverance, too imaginative."

"Too imaginative" meant that she lied, but "lacking perseverance" was worse. How angry Maman had been! Natalie felt a burst of resentment toward her teacher. Why did Mademoiselle need to upset Maman? Since then, Natalie had always made A's in composition, though her other grades sometimes weren't as good.

Georgette was waiting for her on the cement playground. Their walk home took half an hour, and they dragged their feet into the dry Plane tree leaves that preceded the winter. Georgette's house was first, so then Natalie walked alone down her tree-lined avenue.

There was a new door in her back garden that led into the neighbor's yard. Maman was to use it to run away if they came to arrest her. Hélène had told Natalie how they had come for Madame Kahn, at home with two babies who were taken away in another truck. Natalie didn't want to think about it. It was so upsetting. She walked over the clover blooming pink under the laundry lines at the back of the house. From the gate, she noticed that the garage, where Maman kept the bicycle, was shut.

As soon as Natalie opened the entryway door she saw Maman's shawl, hung on the banister with the Jewish badge stitched to it. The webbed stitching of the Star of David caught the light and the black letters *Juif* at its yellow center seemed trapped in the works of a horrible spider.

What would she do if she didn't find Maman's shawl there? What if Maman didn't come back one day? Were there safe places left? What if little Lilla cried and refused to leave? Would Lilla be sent to Switzerland as a refugee? Where would she and Hélène end up? Would they stay together? How would Maman find them after the war? What if the war never ended?

Natalie imagined the girls in her class old and white-haired, dressed in black, a few of them shuffling with a cane, and the war still not ended. In her mind, their faces looked as they did today because it was impossible to imagine them with wrinkles.

What about Father Raoul? It was odd, the way he walked in tiny steps. There was something wrong with his feet. Was he in the Resistance? He couldn't be. Catholics had to love everyone, even their enemies. One good thing about being Jewish was that you didn't have to pray for the Nazis.

Natalie threw her school bag under the coat rack and sat on the worn stairs, hands on her cheeks, thinking about the young man who had crawled into crevices in the Alps to help her and other people escape into Switzerland. He was in the Resistance, older and taller than she, but only a boy. A pity she wasn't old enough. She would have liked to carry secret messages. She kicked off her wood-soled shoes, rummaging for her slippers before starting her homework.

Maman asked where she'd been.

"I walked Georgette home and then I came straight here."

"I warned you!" Maman said, frowning as she always did when Georgette was mentioned. She stood by the window where extravagant Jacobean tulips and peony roses grew on the curtains. "It's common knowledge that her parents fraternize with the Germans. The Mercinars boast about it. Why do you ignore it?"

Natalie hung her head.

"Well," Maman said, "It's no concern of ours. Do your homework, Hélène. Natalie, do yours, and then set the table. We'll eat dinner early. Lilla, see if you can find that yellow pullover with the brown trim. I'll unravel it after dinner. If I wash the yarn and wring it well, the wool can dry tomorrow on the line if it's sunny." She returned to her typing practice, when no one must make a sound or interrupt her.

Wool had disappeared from the market, so had rice, most meat, noodles, biscuits and butter, tinned food, flour, potatoes, chocolate, oil, and lard. This was their third week without meat, fish or eggs. There was no cheese either. Natalie said nothing, but she remembered the delicious dishes Edith had prepared and served twice a day in Switzerland.

Once in a while, someone left a single egg during the night in the letterbox. They had no idea who'd left it. Maman made pancakes with the one egg, without fat or milk, to eat with boiled rutabagas or cabbage. The pancakes were covered in leopard spots where they stuck to the frying pan. They weren't like the airy pancakes Maman used to make when Papa lived with them, but it was food and they were hungry.

For dessert, they ate plums, stewed for hours when the gas was on, with grapes to sweeten them because they'd used up their sugar rations by the first week of the month.

Maman drank the water from boiling turnips or rutabagas for breakfast so that Hélène could eat a second slice of bread each day. She was sixteen and always hungry. The furnace was turned off since there was hardly any coal left. Maman kept a tiny reserve in case one of them became sick. Because it was so cold, the few scarce potatoes froze in the basement. Gelatinous and gray, they had a nasty taste.

They had taken to wearing their coats indoors as well as out. That night, as most nights after dinner, the bread bags with red initials hung at the back of each dining room chair, deflated: their single daily slice had been devoured hours ago.

"In Montreux, we ate sliced bananas with stewed plums," Natalie, who wanted to talk about Papa, told her sisters, hoping that would start the conversation.

"There are no bananas in Switzerland," Hélène said, elbows on the table.

Natalie said, "Yes, there are!"

"Not possible."

"Yes," Natalie insisted, "you weren't there!"

"Impossible."

Lilla interrupted, "Maman, what's a banana?" Lilla's ignorance left her sisters speechless. "Will you get me a banana, Maman?"

"If I could, I would," Maman said, getting up from the table. She was turning a jacket inside out, picking out the seams because the fabric, thin from wear, had faded on the right side.

"Do you remember oranges, Lil?" Maman asked.

"No." Lilla shook her head. "Do we need coupons for oranges?"

"Of course, dummy," Hélène and Natalie said at the same time.

Oranges, grapefruits, lemons, tangerines, bananas, pineapples, all had all vanished from the shops.

Hélène cleared the table. "When the war is over, we will eat tangerines every day," she declared as she pretended to start her homework. Instead, she drew pyramids of orange globes and yellow crescent shapes on the cover of her natural science book.

Maman wiped the oilcloth clean before spreading her bedroom curtains on the table to make a new dress for Hélène, who was growing out of her clothes. Maman grouped her sewing projects to take advantage of the irregular electric current that sometimes blinked twice or vanished without warning.

"No coupons for oranges. Or bananas. Or any tropical fruit," Maman said. She folded her fabric, matched corners, and measured Hélène twice, taking notes. She pushed pins, regularly spaced, into and out of layers of fabric. The heads of the pins made bumps like the trail Hansel and Gretel dropped behind them in the woods to find their way home.

Had Hansel and Gretel been making a sort of map?

Natalie wondered. Better not to ask, because someone was sure to demand where she got the idea. Better to think about tropical fruit.

Tropical fruit sounded so delicious that Natalie was hungry again. The shops sold apples or winter pears from time to time, hard ones that never softened, even though Maman tried to ripen them between two cushions for days. They had to be simmered on top of the stove when the gas was available.

Natalie was drawing the growth stages of a kidney bean she'd nursed in a saucer on a bed of wet shredded rags. Without raising her head, she said, "In Switzerland, we had oranges. Cherries too. Lots of them. And chocolate."

Hélène pushed her chair back. "Stop bragging about Switzerland and having all the fun!" Natalie held her tongue until her bean stock had leaves. "You're jealous, Hélène, I can tell."

She felt guilty for the good food Edith had served, and all the second helpings of cheese and bread and desserts she had enjoyed in Switzerland. A few times, she'd wanted to talk to Hélène about Hans, but she decided against it. Hélène would make fun of the whole thing. Natalie wondered whether Hans would change. He had been her friend for a while, but at the same time, he kept telling her lies. Why? And why so many?

"Silence, all of you," Maman scolded, picking up her scissors. "I've enough on my mind without putting up with your squabbles." As soon as her scissors touched the fabric, the electricity went out. "The third time this evening! Are you done with your homework?" Maman asked, setting a candle on the table.

Faces were a yellowish-gray. Textbook pages were gray. It was impossible to read the school books. If the light came back, they could finish their homework. Otherwise, like yesterday, they would go to bed in the dark and return to school with their work half-done at best.

Natalie thought of Pierre, coming with his stepladder to replace light bulbs in Montreux.

"Look at your long face," Hélène teased.

"I don't have a long face. You do!" Natalie shot back. She was thinking about Papa, and how she had not said goodbye, even though she had been at Tante Pauline's when he died. Stupid Hélène, believing she had had nothing but fun in Switzerland, just like Oncle Marc and Tante Pauline. Natalie shouted, "And you eat Maman's only bread slice every morning! Do you think that's fair?"

Hélène got up from the table. She stood in front of Natalie as if to pummel her. Instead, she shouted, "Dress up time!"

Natalie and Lilla sprang to action and ran to the basement, where Maman's trunk of old clothes waited for them. She had long ago taken out the good fabric to make new clothes. Time to select new roles with matching names. Papa had loved puns. Now Hélène and Natalie had fun, inventing names for their dress-up characters. Wrapped in Maman's Indian shawls, old dropped waist dresses, corsets and anything not yet reused or transformed, the sisters pranced around.

"Hélène," Natalie remembered, "You promised to help me draw skates."

"Tell your mistress not yet, too much to do, Duchess Pazenkor Tropafere has come for tea." Hélène held out her hand to drop a nonexistent visiting card from Mrs.Too-Much-To-Do into an invisible silver tray Natalie-the-maid held at the door.

Natalie peered inside her palm. "This way, please,

Madame la Duchesse."

"Here is your tip," the Duchess said, picking up an old dictionary and thrusting it into Natalie's hands.

"Madame la Duchesse is most generous," Natalie said, dropping the dictionary on a chair. She made a face, bowed, and returned to the trunk, and plunked a perforated top hat over her black braids.

"Docteur Jean-Veut-Pas," she announced. "Here's my card. I'm invited to tea, but I refuse to sit next to that Nazi woman."

"What Nazi woman?" Lilla asked, steadying a purple hat backward on her head.

"You! Frau Maufaitan—Mrs. Foul Weather."

"I'm not Madame Foul Weather!" Lilla's howled, letting her hat slip to the back of her head, its veil a toupee on her forehead. "You are the Nazi-Bad-Weather woman! I'll be Mademoiselle Rigolo. Miss Funny. Maman says it's slang."

"No," Hélène decided, "You are a dancer—Annie Versaire—Anniversary. Or dear Monsieur Itticks."

"Ittick, who's that?" Lilla asked.

"Don't you know anything? Paul Itticks—politics! The food minister. Famous all over the world. Hurry up, Lil, choose."

Upstairs, Natalie introduced the minister. Maman laughed her rare laugh. In the dark, for a few minutes before the erratic electricity returned, they had a good time.

Chapter 36

The Teacher's Visit

The next day, as they were eating dinner in the evening's gray light, Natalie heard footsteps. She raised her hand, the agreed sign to silently warn Maman that someone was coming. Before Maman could run out the back door, Natalie's language teacher, her body concealed in a grey cloak, erupted into the dining room.

Without greetings, Mademoiselle Leblanc declared, "This door of yours is well oiled. To make escaping an easy task, I should think."

"Mademoiselle, come in," said Maman, and motioned the teacher to the sitting room, dismissing the children with a wave of her hand. The darkening sunset deepened to an orange glow.

Mademoiselle walked to the sitting room ahead of Maman. "I want the children present," she commanded.

So the girls followed single file behind Maman, who took a seat in the yellow armchair. Mademoiselle sat opposite her in Papa's leather armchair without being asked.

Why has Mademoiselle come? Natalie and Hélène asked each other with raised eyebrows.

Pale circles showed on the wallpaper by the bookshelf. "Your pewter plates have gone into hiding. Or did you already surrender them to the Metal Collection Center?" the teacher asked.

"I don't know what you mean," Maman replied.

"There were fine plates on this wall when I came to visit after my appointment," Mademoiselle said. "Three years ago. The only pewter collection in town to compare with yours sat on the Goldstein's breakfront, Avenue Victor Hugo. Joseph Goldstein. Well, I didn't come to talk about people who fled to the comfort of other continents, nor to comment on the Fuehrer's need to replenish his supply of cannon balls. Let's get down to business."

Maman looked stiff. "Let's."

"Who is Kleber?"

"What a name!" Maman said, eyes wide. "I have no idea."

"Isn't he the children's older brother?"

Natalie bit her knuckles.

"Years ago, I had hoped for a son," Maman said, "but there are only three girls and myself in this family."

"Where is the wireless?"

"I never bought one." Maman passed her hand on the back of her neck. "Is this about a program you wished the children to listen to?"

Mademoiselle did not answer. "How is it that you listen to the BBC?" she asked, her teeth flashing white in the semi-darkness. "Jews aren't allowed radios."

"Look," Maman said, grabbing the armrests, her face reddening. "As a language teacher in a large high school, I would have thought you'd be too busy to walk unannounced into my home, asking extraordinary questions! From now on, kindly keep to school matters." She let go of the yellow chair's armrests.

"Very well. I brought an excellent essay written by one of your daughters."

The teacher thrust a hand with crimson painted nails out from under her cape. Natalie saw the composition she had handed in the day before. On the top sheet, was a large red question mark. Lower down, were a few red crosses.

Lilla sniffed instead of blowing her nose. Natalie looked down.

In a puzzled voice, Maman began to read, "Now Kleber is back. My big brother is very brave. He ran away from his POW camp. Maman gave him permission to buy a wireless. So he did it in secret because he knows where to go. Now we can listen to the BBC news every night. We lock the doors and close the windows because of the neighbors. We sit down, and Maman throws the Star of David on her scarf in the wastepaper basket."

The dirty word was out. Maman stumbled over it, but took hold of herself and continued. "—Star of David in the wastepaper basket. We listen to messages in code. We know what they mean because Kleber is in the Resistance, and he tells us. When I grow up, we will win the war, and I will come back to explain the secret radio messages. Kleber says we're going to win, even if it takes a long time. But he says the war is going to end soon. We listen to good news coming from friendly countries that we will visit during vacations after the war. That's how we spend a happy evening."

Maman's voice had become deep, guttural.

"Water, for Maman," Natalie mumbled. She couldn't move to fetch it, but only water mattered. With water, she felt, everything would be better.

Lilla moaned, asleep on the sofa. Maman didn't put down the incriminating composition, or perhaps she was no longer aware of it. She stared ahead, the composition trembling in her hand for everyone to see.

Mademoiselle broke the silence. "You're a little shaken and it's understandable. However, you cannot deny this composition is Natalie's work."

Her crimson fingernail pointed to Natalie's name at the top of the page. "We agree this is excellent work for a twelve-year-old. But tell me, where do you think it could take you?" The teacher closed her eyes. "Would some neighbors enjoy it? Or perhaps some, some specialized agency?"

Natalie stood still. No one spoke to her. No one seemed to see her, so that she felt absent and present at the same time because everything was both true and untrue.

Mademoiselle plucked the composition from Maman's hand. "I hold in my hand two hundred francs—a treasure. Dropped into a mailbox or, better still, delivered in person, just think! Two meals at Maxim's, or…?"

Maman rose, a head taller than the teacher, she stood looking down at her. She asked coldly, "What exactly do you intend to do?"

Unable to face the answer, Natalie ran to the kitchen. Forgetting to turn on the light, she retched over the sink. Hélène came in after her.

"Georgette," Natalie gasped. "I hate her. I hope she gets run over. I hope she burns alive. With her horrid curls. I hope she drowns."

"How does Georgette know?" Hélène asked.

"She read a page of my draft."

"What an idiot you are," Hélène said. "Now you need to calm down." She put an arm over Natalie's shoulders. "It'll be all right."

Natalie couldn't bring a full glass of water to Maman because she shook too much.

They went back to the sitting room.

Lilla coughed.

Mademoiselle had grabbed Maman by the wrist and held onto her. "*Jésus-Marie-Mére-de-Dieu*," she said, as if it were one word, her voice urgent and chiding, "I repeat, I have no intention of doing anything at all. I simply wanted to give you a very stern warning. Talk to the child. Teach her. Teach the three of them to trust no one but you, and never, ever, to confide on paper."

Maman sat, breathing fast.

"By the way," Mademoiselle Leblanc said, "I brought you my meat coupons and my sugar ration tickets for which, as a diabetic, I have no use. That's all." She placed the coupons on Maman's armrest.

Natalie felt no better. "I hate Georgette. I will never speak to her again," she sobbed, and found relief in the thought that the trouble was all Georgette's fault. No one said a word.

Mademoiselle let herself out through the front door without farewell. She had to walk around the house to retrieve her bicycle.

Natalie cautiously huddled with her family. She'd wanted so much to write the best essay so Maman would be proud of her, and her attempt to help nasty Georgette had landed her in trouble. She never managed to do anything right. In Montreux, when she tried to please Skinna—even making her a bouquet of wildflowers—she failed, however hard she tried. That must be why nobody loved her.

Natalie looked at Maman, hugging Hélène and Lilla on either side of her. Through the window behind them, Natalie watched her teacher—hands on the high handlebars, her back straight, wrapped in her indestructible loden cloak—cycling away into the unlit street. After a while, she could no longer see her. Still she watched.

Natalie caught a glimpse of Maman. Her teeth biting her lower lip for a long time.

"What on earth were you thinking!" she finally exclaimed.

Natalie looked down. She had so enjoyed inventing an

older brother. “I wanted...I wanted to get the best grade,” she stammered, filled with shame, forgetting to add, “for you.”

Maman shrugged. “Next time, better aim for a failing grade.”

Chapter 37

In the Garage

Two weeks later, Maman let Natalie stay home from school since she had a tummy ache. She spoke of asking the doctor to come, but most doctors didn't visit Jewish homes anymore and they didn't want Jews in their waiting rooms. Jewish doctors were forbidden to practice and had all vanished.

Natalie was tired of being indoors. She took her favorite book, *The Three Musketeers*, into the garage to read in peace. Discarded furniture, piled under oilcloth remnants and old blankets, filled the back of the garage. She found the short-legged chair that Maman had used years ago when she nursed Lilla, and sat down in front of the barrage of furniture that made a fine barricade for reading. The musketeers must have had maps and learned them by heart because they were never lost. D'Artagnan loved one of the queen's women.

The garage door, which Natalie had not bothered to close properly, squeaked open. Without getting up, she kicked it shut. She wanted to read about D'Artagnan's love for Madame Bonnacieux, who'd vanished without a trace. In spite of his best efforts, D'Artagnan couldn't find her. Madame Bonnacieux was married to a mean, stupid man. He and Cardinal Richelieu, who hated the queen, were responsible for her disappearance.

Natalie heard scraping on the cement floor. She got up, expecting a cat to jump off the three-legged table behind her and amble out. There was no cat. Level with her face, a pair of eyes stared at her through the slats of garden chairs. Human eyes. Natalie turned to run.

"Help me get out," a rasping voice said from behind the furniture.

"I'll scream, if you try to hurt me," Natalie said, clutching her book about brave men.

"You mustn't tell anyone about me. Promise?"

Natalie needed time. "I know why you're in the garage," she said, less afraid because the voice wasn't yet a person. The eyes said nothing. "You're hiding."

"Are you alone?"

"Nooo." It was better never to volunteer information.

"Can you bring me something to eat, Natalie? Anything."

"We don't have much," Natalie said, adding, "How do you know my name?" She held on to her book.

"Have you forgotten your Tante Pauline? Please go and tell your mother I'm here."

"You should be in Switzerland," Natalie said. "Why do you say I must not tell anybody, and then ask me to tell Maman?" She turned away. "I'll see what can be done." People spoke in that careful way nowadays.

Natalie saw Maman entering the garage with her arms crossed. Tante Pauline stepped gingerly out from behind the barricade, dressed in expensive clothes with earrings and bracelets. But there were spider webs on her coat and rips on her stockings. Her hair was untidy, and her face was white.

Maman said, "Natalie tells me you were hiding in the garage."

Without hugging Maman, Tante Pauline said, "Marc was taken yesterday at your railway station. I got away. There were no more trains, and I had nowhere to go before curfew. The garage was unlocked. So, I slept there."

"Why on earth didn't you knock on the front door?"

"I was going to, after the children left for school. The garage door slammed shut. I thought Natalie had left."

Maman was unsmiling. "You'd better come in." She led the way.

In the sitting room Pauline sat on the sofa and raised her chin, looking from Maman to Natalie, and from Natalie to Maman several times.

"What's the matter, Pauline?" Maman said, her voice dry.

"The two of us had better talk alone," Tante Pauline announced.

"You mean our conversation won't be suitable for a child."

"Exactly," she said, looking more like the old Tante Pauline now that she was leaning against the cushions on the sofa, uncrossing and re-crossing her legs.

"Yet endangering my child's life by making her cross the border illegally was suitable."

Natalie breathed easier. Maman was on her side, not Skinna's.

Pauline said, "We did what was best."

"That won't do." Maman pointed an index finger at Tante Pauline's chest. "You promised Natalie would go to Switzerland by train, in a Red Cross convoy."

"The convoys were full, Noémi."

It felt strange to hear Maman's first name coming from Skinna's mouth.

"I don't have time for arguments," Skinna said, "I need help. I have no money to go home, no papers. Don't you agree one good turn deserves another?"

"What good turn?" Maman burst out, arms flying. "You told me you'd give Francis a message, yet you failed to tell me you'd arranged for my husband to live in your home for the rest of his life."

"He was dying." Skinna looked at the ceiling, her hands joined like a Christian martyr.

"If that's your excuse, it's not a good one."

"He was dying," Skinna repeated.

"And you decided to keep that to yourself, instead of helping me to go to him?"

Pauline wrung her hands. "I'll leave if that's what you want." She remained seated.

Natalie went to the kitchen, leaving the doors open so she might hear. She filled the kettle with water, turned on the gas ring, set two cups and saucers on a tray and added all of the honey from a half-empty small jar. She pretended to be busy, banging lids against pots and opening and closing drawers needlessly, because Maman and Skinna would talk more freely if they thought she was busy. She made chamomile tea, since there was nothing else to offer.

Maman said, "So the child was exposed!"

Skinna replied, "I promise you, Natalie never touched her father."

A lie! What a lie! Both Skinnies told lies. Natalie remembered rushing in and hugging Papa when she first went into his room, and Skinna being upset.

Maman said, "Death isn't only about touching."

"Natalie came home when you wanted her, Noémi. You fly off the handle so easily that you forget I'm in danger," Skinna said.

Natalie approached with the tray.

Maman laughed an ugly laugh. "You, in danger? How

dare you, a Swiss citizen, speak to me of danger!" She put her hands flat on the table, her weight on her arms. "I risk arrest every minute of every day, and you come to me for protection?" She spoke clearly, articulating as if stupid Skinna were deaf. "You know nothing of danger, Pauline, and nothing of worry, either. Let me tell you about worrying. As a mother, for a start, I worry about what will happen to the children, if I am taken."

"Our in-laws have taken precautions," Skinna said, and re-crossed her legs.

"Their plan is to take effect after my arrest?"

"Our father-in-law has contacts. He is—you know who he is as well as I do. He managed to obtain three exemption certificates."

"Papers proving my children aren't Jewish since they're not mine, but their father's children!" Maman kept nodding, but Natalie felt no relief.

Skinna was quick to agree. "Yes, yes. I just told you."

Maman dropped down into her armchair. In a slow voice, she asked, "What about me, Pauline?"

Natalie felt more scared and angry than when the Germans came and raided their home looking for Maman.

Skinna examined her hands. "Those papers are very costly, you see."

Maman sprung up in front of Skinna. "Are you saying my life, the life of their dead son's wife, the mother of their grandchildren, isn't worth some money? That I am not worth saving from the concentration camps we all know about?" Her voice was sharper than her best scissors as she paced in front of Skinna.

Natalie set the tray down by Maman's armchair. She ran back to the kitchen for the teapot, her wood-sole shoes clattering, and returned slowly, putting the heel of one foot against the toes of the other so that, holding the teapot handle with both hands, it took her a while to reach the sitting room. All the while Natalie listened, no longer sure she wanted to hear about her grandparents unwillingness to help Maman, even though they had bought papers to save her and her sisters! And Skinna wanted Maman to be sorry for her, while she had two homes, a passport and money for new clothes whenever she wanted, and Maman was in constant danger of being arrested!

"But, you're a Jew, that would be lying." Skinna said, her voice rising.

Maman stopped pacing long enough to scream, "Does it disqualify me as a mother? Does it select me for a sealed boxcar to Germany? Does it prove I deserve starvation and torture? To have my body thrown to the dogs like butcher's bones? Is that what you want, you solid, kind, loving Christians that you are?"

Natalie felt terrified, appalled by what Maman had described.

Skinna repeated weakly, "I'll leave if that's what you want." Still she remained seated.

"It's the second time you've offered," Maman said in a normal voice. "You should have thought, before coming, that anyone, seeing you creep into a Jewish property, would be justified in assuming you have something to hide."

There was an awful silence before Maman said, "Ah!" as if she'd just noticed Natalie. "Phone Madame Remidoux, Natalie. Thank her for her invitation. Tell her both of us look forward to lunch. Use my exact words."

Natalie went to the hall with a heavy heart. She guessed the lunch invitation didn't include her. How could Madame Remidoux have known there would be two guests for lunch? But Maman had not mentioned an invitation. It meant that Madame Remidoux helped hide people from the Nazis.

Natalie remembered Maman coming home from her Swiss friend's home with a chicken some time ago, and so much makeup on her face that she was hard to recognize.

She also remembered Skinna kissing Papa. Madame Remidoux would refuse to help Skinna if she knew about the kiss. Maman would phone herself if Natalie refused. So she must do as she was told. Besides, if she told Madame Remidoux about the kiss, Maman would hear about it. That would be terrible.

Before she dialed the Remidoux's number, Natalie heard Maman say, "How could you understand? You have no children."

Maman didn't need to remind Skinna that she had no children, Natalie thought, as she waited for the operator. Skinna was stupid. It was useless to explain things to her. Natalie remembered the conversation between Skinna and Papa. She wanted a baby, but Marc didn't want children. Natalie felt sorry for Skinna about that. She couldn't tell Maman because she was willing to help Skinna. Maman was better than Skinna, much, much better.

As she hung up the receiver under the mouthpiece nailed on the wall, Natalie heard Maman ask, "Had Marc already collected the false papers?"

Natalie hurried down the passage and saw Skinna clutching the armrests of her chair.

"We'd only just stepped out of the train, on our way to collect them," Skinna said.

Natalie stood by the door. Neither Maman nor Skinna paid attention to her.

"Why didn't you go back to Paris?" Maman asked.

"I told you," Skinna continued, "Marc was walking

ahead of me. All of a sudden, three men grabbed him and dragged him away. I was so shocked that I dropped my handbag. I didn't dare pick it up. I kept walking. What if they'd noticed me? I had no money on me. Soon, they'd enforce the curfew. I know no one else in this suburb, so I kept on walking till I reached your garage."

"The Germans arrested him?"

"They didn't wear uniforms." Skinna's voice trembled.

"Chamomile?" Maman asked Skinna as she filled her cup from the teapot. "In that case, it's the French Militia. Marc's in for a scare. He'll be all right. Call our beloved father-in-law. With his connections, he'll buy Marc's release. Drink your tea," she said, as if it were tea instead of an herbal infusion. "Then you better hurry up and change clothes. I'm not allowed on the streets all the time."

Minutes later, wearing Mama's raincoat, a scarf over her hair, and an empty handbag on her arm, Skinna walked out, staying several feet behind Maman, who pushed her bicycle along the tree-lined avenue. For Skinna's sake, they mustn't be seen talking together.

Chapter 38

Good Versus Bad People

Natalie no longer wanted to read. The garage had lost its appeal. She drank the leftover chamomile, seeing herself in a white coat, listening to someone's chest with a stethoscope.

Maman was back before Lilla and Hélène came home from school.

"Does Oncle Marc help with false papers?" Natalie asked as Maman closed the door. If he did, he was brave, she thought, still hating him.

Maman said, "I count on you, Natalie, to tell no one about this."

"But, who has those papers?"

"I wish I knew, Natalie. I didn't even think to ask, though you did. You are clever sometimes. But remember, not a word to anyone!"

"Not even to Hélène?"

Maman replied, "If Hélène is asked, I want her to truthfully say she knows nothing."

In the kitchen, Maman filled her bucket with water. On her knees, she angrily pushed her scrub brush back and forth over the faded red tiles as if to remove all trace of color from the floor. She raised her head once. "Remember, Natalie, they have ways to make anyone talk."

Did Maman not care what would happen if the Germans questioned her? No, that wasn't what Maman meant. It meant that Maman trusted her. Natalie felt threatened and proud all at once. She cleared the tea tray.

She washed the cups and saucers, thinking about the way the Nazis forced people to talk. In homes, back alleys, dark churches, cloakrooms, and cafés, people passed on information. Children heard their parents talk. The Nazis coerced details by arresting people, denying them sleep, food, water, visitors and parcels. Worse were the physical threats of beatings, pulling out nails, breaking bones, holding the prisoner's head under water till they suffocated, reviving them, and then doing it again.

That evening, the power was out. After a cold dinner, the girls went to bed early.

The night was cold. Natalie kicked off her wood-soled shoes, crawled under the counterpane, and pulled it up over her face. She wished she could tell Hélène that Skinna had spent a night with the spiders in the garage. She would also have liked to tell her that Marc was arrested at the train station and that he was mean but brave as well.

So far, she'd found people were either good or bad. The heroes in *The Three Musketeers* were good, so was the Queen. The Cardinal was wicked, and so were the Germans. If Marc procured false papers for people, why had he not given any to Maman so that she could go to Papa in Switzerland? How good and how bad was Oncle Marc? Perhaps he was both good and bad. She felt that she was good and bad at the same time. It was very hard to figure out. Nowadays, Hélène had no time for Natalie because she had a new best girlfriend. Natalie wished someone could help her understand.

Chapter 39

Bombing

"Leave me alone, Lilla!" Natalie pleaded from her bed, feeling Lilla tug at her shoulder. But the tugging didn't stop. Liliane often came into Natalie's bed when she had a nightmare. What do you want, Lilla?"

It was still dark outside.

"I hear bumblebees in my room, big ones," whimpered tiny Lilla.

"No bumblebees at night, Lilla. They sleep! Go back to bed," Natalie grumbled.

"Yes, yes, listen, Nat." Lilla climbed under Natalie's covers.

Natalie sat straight up and listened. "I hear your bumblebees," she said. "Very large ones. So large!"

"So large, they are planes?" Lilla asked as she clung to Natalie.

"It's possible," said Natalie.

"I didn't want to tell you, in case it frightened you," Lilla said in the dark. Natalie was touched. She pulled the covers over them both and wrapped her arms around Lilla.

In a clear voice, as if she were asking whether they'd eat breakfast early, Lilla said, "Are we all going to die?"

"No, no, no," Natalie protested to reassure her sister. "Of course not. It's just the noise from plane engines. Plug your ears, and you'll be fine." She watched Lilla curl up on her side, holding a pillow over her face with both hands. Natalie's mind drifted to Wednesday afternoon. Madame Louviers, their talkative next-door neighbor, had told Maman all about living in Morocco for years. Eventually, over the dividing back fence, she had handed Maman her back door key, asking that Natalie come in to feed Fez, their white Siamese cat, during a three-day absence. She and her husband were going to visit their daughter in the country. In exchange, she promised Maman four farm eggs on her return. One for each of them. The Louviers left that afternoon, each carrying an oversized suitcase to fill with hoped-for farm provisions.

Natalie recalled going in twice to feed the blue-eyed cat, and being impressed by the Moroccan plates on the walls, the white arches between the rooms, the Kilim rugs, the blue and red leather poufs, everything there so different from home. Was there a war in Morocco too?

There was a moment of silence before Natalie heard a tiny, shrill whistle coming from far way. It grew louder till it sounded like a drill working into the roof. Groaning, creaking, ear-splitting sounds filled the night. For the last several weeks, planes had come many times, never so close, never so noisy.

"Stay in bed, Lilla," she shouted to make sure to be heard, peeling back the covers on her side of the bed, ready to bolt. She felt compelled to look outside. She raced toward the window. A crisp, cascading sound made her jump back as the glass windowpanes dissolved into gold-edged pellets tinkling at her feet. The cold air slapped her while an endless blasting sound hurt the inside of her ear.

Natalie ran back to the other side of the room for her plaid robe, which hung behind the door. Before she could grab it, the floor lurched under her bare feet as if to sweep her out of the window. She threw her arms across the chest of drawers to stop it from sliding across the floor.

When the room settled, Natalie stared out, ignoring jagged pieces of glass below the window frame. The thudding sounds continued, like furious bumper cars bouncing off each other before flipping upside down on the ground.

Peering out to the left, Natalie was relieved to find the vegetable plot of the policeman intact behind the ivy-covered brick wall. But to the right, in the Louviers' garden, a huge hole gaped in the middle of the lawn. Their oak tree had fallen over the fence separating the two properties. Its canopy was too far to be seen, but its knotted roots stood high, raised up over the crushed fence between the two houses, like snakes about to strike.

"Maman! Maman!" Lilla howled in terror, "I want Maman!"

Maman appeared in her robe, with her hair down. She lifted Liliane. "It's all right, Lilla, only a bomb next door," she explained carefully, as if Lilla were a toddler.

"Where are we going? I want—I want," Lilla stammered, her arms tight around Maman's neck, uncertain what she wanted.

Hélène came in, stretching, her hair tangled. "It's almost midnight. Why are you making such a din, Lilla?" she joked. "Keep it quiet, will you? I'm so tired. I'm going back to bed."

Lilla, cried, "It's not my fault! It's the planes. Ask Natalie if you don't believe me."

"We are all going to the ground floor, girls." Maman interrupted. "If you need to, nap under the dining room table, it's very thick and strong. We'll be closer to the front door if we need to leave. I never thought the time would come when we'd be grateful for the suitcase I've prepared."

A series of detonations caused them all to cover their ears. Maman shouted to be heard.

"Get the pillows and the blankets from my room to share, Hélène."

Maman and Liliane made their way to the ground floor, followed by Hélène, whose head stuck up above her arms full of bedding, and Lilla's Babar the Elephant in his bright green suit under her chin.

Natalie, wearing her robe over her double layer of pajamas, found her slippers. With the blotter from her desk, she pushed the broken glass on the floor aside and stood mesmerized at her window. The night had split open, pouring light as bright as morning into her room.

Looking over at her bed, she saw Papa's painting, slightly askew. She studied the scene of a mosque with its dawn sky in graduated blues and coral pink, and opposite the mosque, her mirror, hanging at a crazy angle. Though it was night, she clearly saw the green and blue clothes she intended to wear to school in the morning, her socks mended at the toe and the heel, and her frayed shoelaces.

Outside the world was illuminated, too. The Louviers' house was enveloped by flames, twisting like a cordon of insane monkeys.

The neighbor's house leaned forward, then rolled back, shrinking like melting sugar, as windows blew open, disgorging flowers and shelves and flowerpots, as it shed its chimney. Natalie covered her ears against the vibrations.

Black smoke with grey edges rose and widened, drifting toward her like an advancing tide. The Louviers house collapsed with a roar. Natalie brought her hands down to cover her nose with her sleeve, watching stones tumble and pipes twist outward. Burning chunks of unrecognizable material tumbled around the spot where a home had stood, and was soon covered by debris.

Hélène came upstairs to watch with her. "It stinks!" Hélène exclaimed.

Maman called in her angriest voice, "Come down, the two of you, right away! Down here to the dining room where we can wait together in case the planes return. They sometimes do. And wait there for me."

Natalie and Hélène joined Lilla.

Maman reappeared, dressed, startlingly calm. "We're unbelievably fortunate, children! Incredibly fortunate."

"What's fortunate about bombing?" Natalie asked. Had Maman gone mad from the noise and smoke and fear?

"Of course! Most fortunate! Don't you see? If our house had been hit, we'd be on the street."

"People can't live on the street?" Lilla asked reasonably. "Why, Maman?"

"You'd be taken to an orphanage, children. Where else?" Maman answered, looking anxious again.

"Wouldn't you come with us?" Lilla asked, pressing herself against Maman's skirt, who, for once, didn't seem aware of her.

"An orphanage is for children, not their parents," she said, arms crossed, hugging her own shoulders.

Natalie and Hélène exchanged a look. No one would publicly help Maman if the house fell, because she was a Jew. The Germans would get her.

"If the planes come back, are we next?" Lilla asked.

"That's not what I mean, darling," Maman said, stroking Lilla's hair.

"Don't speak of it, Lilla. It'll bring bad luck," Hélène said.

"You say I'm wrong all the time, Hélène! That's mean.

I was only asking!" Lilla squealed.

The faltering electric light briefly came back on, and then went off. The house was dark, though the night was once again quiet.

Maman said, "Natalie, run to the kitchen and fill the kettle and the largest pan with water."

Natalie did as she was told. At least, there'd be water to drink—cold water, since they had no gas for the stove. Slowly, a trickle of water filled the kettle and their largest pan.

When the firemen finally arrived, they appeared as bulky silhouettes with helmets in the light from the blazes, as they climbed their ladders and entered the Louviers' home. They threw out what could be heaved through doors or windows and directed so many jets of water inside and out that there were puddles everywhere. Water gathered around lanterns, on chairs, poufs, the rugs dropped pell-mell onto smashed flower beds, broken shrubs, and wrecked lawns. Ashes spread onto the trees, onto household debris, on the roofs of nearby houses, their own neglected garden, the mailboxes, and windowsills.

Outside, the Louviers' broken dishes now lay on splattered sheets. A man's suit jacket was stabbed by a serving fork. A painting lay, half stuck into the face of a fallen grandfather clock. A sewing machine waited upside down next to chairs, drapes, cushions soaked in mud, twisted 78 rpm records, and a torn carton of shiny pictures with curled-up edges—family photographs, Natalie guessed. On top of ash-covered costumed dolls on the path, there was a drum, smashed by a wrought iron fire screen, and lots of pill bottles.

The soaking and gutting lasted for hours. Natalie found it impossible not to watch.

When the firemen left, thin smoke still rose from the

rubble. The firefighters were followed by three sturdy young men with white armbands, who started digging with shovels and picks, filling sacks. Firemen helpers, Natalie thought, watching them kick uneven lumps of rubble apart before leaning over the debris with gloved hands, pulling a ladle here, a kettle there, an unbroken cup, a hammer, silk ties, a toaster, and a bicycle pump from the remains.

Natalie looked away a second. When she looked up again, the young men were stuffing pots, jars, and tools into their bags. One of them pulled on a white furry strip.

Lilla screamed, "There's Fez!"

"Who?" Maman asked, getting out her handkerchief. A new, acrid smoke, shaped like a mushroom, was bringing out the smell of burned garbage.

"Fez! The cat! Madame Louviers' cat!" Lilla cried, pulling off the handkerchief from her nose. "Poor Fez! I want him. I'll take care of him for Madame Louviers. Agreed, Maman?"

But the furry white tail was not attached to Fez. The young man threw the tail behind him and kept searching. Natalie ran indoors. She could no longer watch.

When, at eight o'clock, two policemen on rusty bicycles arrived, each boy with an armband slung his bags over his shoulder and left at a trot in the opposite direction. Natalie felt wide-awake, though her eyes hurt from the smoke. From the blue armchair in the living room, she heard a knock on the front door. It was the police.

Maman waited for the men in the hallway where she was not required to wear her Star of David badge. She proved unable to help the police when she couldn't tell them where the owners of the villa had gone.

Maman said nothing about Natalie going next door to feed the cat, or about the promised four eggs. The policeman explained that there had also been bomb explosions near the train station. They had worked through the night. As for the gas, water, and electricity, they were cut for safety reasons. He didn't know when they would be restored. Maman promised to inform them promptly if she received information about the Louviers.

In their almost intact house, Lilla had fallen asleep on a corner of the sitting room rug, with Babar on her tummy. Maman tried to reach the Relief Office by phone. Natalie waited for volunteers to board up her now useless window.

Chapter 40

Christmas

It was December again. December 1943. There were no geese, lambs, ducks, hams or roasts at the butcher's for Christmas. Not even fake ones hung in the window of his shop. Maman said it was just as well, because they would have been priced out of reach.

Maman bought a broken pine branch, put it in a bucket with some soil from the garden, and hoisted it onto a table to make it look taller. It was a reasonable Christmas tree, though it was lopsided. She decorated it with the painted glass birds, bells, and tinsel she kept in Papa's wardrobe. A neighbor gave them half of a skinned rabbit and Maman made a stew with it. There was a whole potato for each of them, with canned peaches for dessert. She measured a teaspoon of evaporated milk over each of their bowls because it was the last tin of her reserve. She needed to make it last.

Maman had traded her wine coupons for candy so that the sisters received a candy bar of flour and sugar covered with a layer of chocolate so thin that the filling showed through. Still, it was a treat.

While the girls were away at school, Maman had made each of them a skirt out of a blue blanket as a Christmas present. The skirts were trimmed with bright braid remnants a dressmaker had given Maman in exchange for Papa's miniature tools that the dressmaker could use to repair her sewing machine. Hélène's skirt had four pleats in front and came with a bolero. Natalie's had two pleats, and a pocket. Lilla's had a hollow pleat front and back, and two pockets. Maman had even made a tiny skirt for Lilla's doll. After opening their presents, they stood by the Christmas tree to sing the carols they sang with Papa every Christmas, even his favorite, "Angels in the Countryside."

If only angels sang in the countryside! Natalie sang along because she was expected to, but she felt tearful.

Hélène wanted to sing a favored song about French troops with spirited lyrics: "Do you hear in the countryside, the roar of those blood-thirsty soldiers?"

But Maman said no, singing "La Marseillaise" was forbidden. It was no longer the national song of France. If someone reported them, they would all be arrested.

Without Papa, no Christmas could be happy. Natalie doubted that angels were real. She'd never seen one, let alone heard one sing. If they existed, they too must be afraid of the Germans.

At dinnertime, Natalie readied to pour water into their glasses, as usual. There was a crackling layer of ice in the water pitcher on the sideboard. Maman sent the girls to bed early because of the cold. There was no coal left for the furnace.

During the holidays, Maman let Hélène and Natalie take turns going to the playground in the municipal park. Lilla wasn't allowed out because she kept getting sore throats and bronchitis. Hélène and Natalie took turns playing at home with her. With the pond frozen, children skated with or without skates. When the weather was milder, they played netball, hide and seek, or cops-and-robbers. An older girl at the swings asked Natalie whether she'd eaten rabbit stew on Christmas day.

"I don't remember," Natalie lied, thinking of the tough gray meat they had eaten.

"You're lying! You ate it and that was not rabbit, you fool! You ate cat meat. So what? Don't make a face! We did too. It's meat. My papa's a policeman. He knows. He says that's why there are no cats around."

Another girl agreed. "My uncle's a vet. He looked at the bones and said they were cat bones. When he told the butcher, the butcher shrugged."

Natalie was glad she hadn't known. She wouldn't have eaten it. It was too disgusting to think about so she wouldn't tell anyone at home.

Chapter 41

Grenade

On the last day of the Christmas vacation under a gray sky, Natalie hurried to the playground, carrying the green ball she'd found in a moleskin trunk in the basement. A man in a beret rode a bicycle with a hoe and a rake tied to the central bar. He called out as if he knew her well.

"Hello, Natalie! Going to the playground?"

She thought he must be the father of one of the playground children, so she nodded. Without leaving his bike, he scooped the ball away from her and twirled it in the air with one hand.

"It's mine! Give it back!" she cried.

He wasn't going fast, doing wide zigzags in the street, so Natalie kept up with him.

"I'll give it back to you in a minute," He said, and slipped her ball into the bicycle's front metal basket.

"All you have to do is to roll my ball down the street when I tell you. Will you do that? After we turn the corner, when you reach the house with the Swastika flag, roll it across the street, and you can have your ball back. Ok, Natalie?"

It sounded easy enough. Natalie ran beside him. The man pulled another ball from the front of his shirt and slid it into her outstretched hands. It was smaller and much heavier than hers. And a different shape than round. She held it in both hands as she ran down the street. Her heartbeat was loud in her ears, as if the thumping could be heard in the street.

She turned the corner and a couple of blocks ahead on her right saw the house requisitioned by the German Kommandantur, with the flapping Swastika flag on the facade, and two sentry boxes. The playground was seven blocks beyond the house. Now the man with the gardening tools pedaled slightly ahead of her. Natalie kept trotting, holding his ball against her chest. Far away at the park, she heard the girls' shouts—something indistinct that sounded like, "Come on! Come on!" It helped her to keep running.

Just ahead of her, a black car slowed to a stop at the curb. Natalie hesitated. The man on the bicycle hissed at her, "Drop it. Now! Jesus, drop it!" Then he pedaled away.

Natalie heard the threat in his voice. Across from the house with the spider-black Swastika flag, she crouched, and let the ball roll toward the car. A German officer in a long coat with silver signs on his collar stepped out, looked at her, and smiled with one side of his mouth. She recognized him as the officer who'd come to the house looking for Maman. She had told him that Maman was in the hospital. When he had turned on his heel, she'd been proud of her lie. But now she was afraid, feeling cold and sweaty all over.

The officer took a step next to the shrub on the sidewalk before bending toward the rolling ball, his gloved right hand held out. Natalie was already running, but she glanced back once, long enough to see lightning.

Natalie fell against a fence, her ears aching inside her head, worse than when her neighbor's house had been bombed. She clamped her hands over them. On the sidewalk across the street, under necklaces of glass beads, a Christmas tree suddenly lit up where a shrub had been. Shreds of fabric with buttons and fingers hung from it. Natalie ran again, her legs worked faster. She continued toward the park, minutes away, without feeling in any part of her body. The schoolgirls on the playground had hold of her green ball and tossed it further and further. She couldn't hear the girls, but she saw them scattering and running away.

1944

Chapter 42

Hostages

Apart from the explosion Natalie had caused in front of the German-occupied villa, it seemed that life had been quiet during the Christmas vacation. Natalie's hearing slowly improved. But when school started again in January 1944, Natalie discovered that her teacher from elementary school, Madame Leverdier, was absent. Her class had a replacement teacher.

Sylviane, who sat on Natalie's left, confided in a murmur that Madame Leverdier's seventeen-year-old son, Dennis, had been shot dead by the Germans. Three days after Christmas, a German officer had been found bleeding in a sentry box. No one knew where. But the Germans had grabbed six men at random, including Dennis, who'd stepped out to buy apples for his mother.

The Germans had driven their prisoners away. On New Year's Day at dawn, they had shot Dennis and the men in reprisal at the Mont Valérien prison. The French police were ordered to remove the bodies and clean up the mess. People used to tell Madame Leverdier that Dennis, with his limp, was fortunate, since his handicap kept him out of compulsory work camps in Germany.

Natalie refused to let the news sink in. But at home, alone in the sitting room, she felt appalled and closed her eyes. Behind her eyelids she imagined the hospital doctors discovering that the six men brought in by the police weren't dead. They had only fainted from loss of blood. After eating black-market food and resting in a secret place near the sea in Normandy, they were improving. Friends told their families that under their bandages, Dennis and the wounded men were recovering. Even the German officer that Natalie thought she had killed was doing better.

How could she have killed him? She had not even touched him. Was she a criminal? Should she be happy there was one less Nazi alive? Was the officer dead, or was he safe inside the house he'd confiscated from a French family? There was nothing in the newspapers about taking the men prisoner for having killed an officer. She could not be sure. She wished Papa were there so she could confide in him. She knew she would remember rolling the ball toward the car when the Nazi officer stepped out, and the dreadful feeling in her ears for the rest of her life—and the noise that had knocked her down against the fence. Catholic girls could go to their parish priest, and with three Ave Marias, God would forgive them. They were free to go on with their lives. She hated all Nazis, of course, but she had not meant to kill one. That event, and the tree-trunk man were the worse part of the war for her.

Chapter 43

A Raid

Lilla had pneumonia again. A neighbor had taken her to the hospital so Maman could stay home in relative safety. It was sad to set the table with only three plates. Natalie missed Lilla, who never stopped playing, in spite of all, as if the Germans had never come.

After supper, Natalie, Hélène, and Maman were doing the dishes when a cavalcade of boots thundered up the front steps. Someone rang the bell, shaking and kicking the front door. Maman untied her apron, grabbed her shawl from the banister and slipped away toward the basement stairs.

"Open the door, Nat." Hélène pushed her out of the kitchen. With a galloping heart, Natalie opened the front door.

"Madame is to come!" An immense German in a black uniform bellowed above her as he marched into the house.

Natalie stared up at him. "Maman's at the clinic. We're doing dishes," she said, unable to think of a new lie, holding the dishcloth high enough for him to see.

Hélène crept up behind her. The officer back-handed them against the wall, yelling in German as he led in a storm of men-in-black who pointed revolvers as they spread throughout the house.

As soon as the officer strode into the sitting room to the right, Natalie and Hélène rushed to the dining room.

They each slid behind a heavy curtain with enormous flowers. Peering out, Natalie saw a covered military truck at the gate, its engine running. Two soldiers with rifles guarded the back. Holding her breath, Natalie listened for a long time to heavy footsteps, banging and thumping, and things falling down the stairs in a cascade of noise, as Germans throughout the house shouted to each other.

At the sound of a shrill whistle, the armed men ran outside in a tight group and climbed into the truck, which roared away. The house, full of echoes, slowly fell silent. Immobile at first behind the drapes, Natalie and Hélène emerged and faced each other.

Had they killed Maman? Wordlessly, they explored the house on tiptoes. The clothes cupboard door in the hallway was torn off its hinges and thrown to the floor, as were cake pans, glass jars, rags, and pieces of the broom handle. Furniture was overturned. Books with their spines broken were kicked into corners. Strips of wallpaper hung from the stairwell walls. Their plaid dressing gowns, which usually hung over two pairs of pajamas, now lay like headless corpses at odd angles on the landing. Trampled underpants and petticoats were covered by glass spikes from broken picture frames. Kapok bloomed from slits on mattresses dragged off the box springs.

With throats so dry they couldn't talk, Natalie and Hélène hesitantly made their way back to the kitchen where they'd last been with Maman.

They stopped at the door. Maman, or an apparition of her, stood at the sink, one hand submerged in the water basin, the other slowly moving in and out, endlessly washing the blue striped bowl.

"Maman," Hélène whispered, "where were you?"

Natalie grabbed her elbow and pulled her back into the

hallway. "Don't ask!" she hissed. "It's better if we don't know. If they ask us, we can tell the truth."

"They don't deserve it," Hélène cried in a strangled voice.

"No, but they have ways to make people talk," Natalie said.

They cleared a path to the bedrooms before a power failure could prevent them. Wastepaper baskets in hand, they delicately picked up splintered glass off the landing. The headless pajama people returned to the wardrobes, mended underwear and socks fell into drawers that were scattered about. Natalie helped Hélène heave mattresses back onto their beds, leaving the rips unstitched, out of sight on the underside.

They remade the beds together, stuffing pillows back into pillowslips. Tomorrow they would push the furniture back against the walls. There was no squabbling. Repairs would have to wait until after the war. Natalie kept telling herself it didn't matter, because Maman had found a secret hiding place. For once, she slept without dreams.

Chapter 44

Kindness Coupons

Returning home from Sunday school at the Protestant Church Hélène asked, "Nat, did you notice? The Mercinars are repainting their house."

"And they have a fountain on their lawn," Natalie volunteered, wondering whether Georgette, whom she'd avoided all the winter, knew of the German raid on their home.

Hélène said, "Where did Monsieur Mercinar find the money for all this? Maman said he's only a secretary at the City Hall."

Natalie didn't answer. Everyone knew the Mercinars gave parties for German officers.

In Maman's garden, gravel sank into the paths. Dandelions and other weeds grew on what used to be lawns before being planted with long-harvested potatoes. Maman had no money for a gardener.

Inside the house, the wallpaper remained scarred. A greenish undercoating of paint showed like milky seaweed trails where Maman had tried to glue the wallpaper back in place. The parquet flooring was dull from lack of wax. In the kitchen an empty space reminded them where the refrigerator once stood. Maman had exchanged it for a wheelbarrow full of potatoes.

Outside, it was frigid. The snow, at first wet, had frozen and thawed again. There was no sun, only a white hole in the sky. Natalie and her sisters wore their overcoats and knitted hats indoors and out because snow and ice covered most of the area and they didn't have logs for the furnace or the fireplace. They wore their gloves to do their homework and Maman practiced typing at the dining room table wearing gloves with the fingertips cut out.

On Easter Sunday, though no mail was delivered, Natalie spotted an envelope glowing white through the window of the letterbox at the gate. She lifted it out. There was no name or address. A letter from Rosie? Pulling off her glove, she used an index finger to tear it open on her way to the house.

There was no message, only a few coupons like tiny stamps at the bottom. "An anonymous letter," Natalie said, handing Maman the envelope.

"Coupons. Mmm. Enough for a small loaf of bread, half a liter of milk, and a bar of soap," Maman said, lifting out the small colored squares.

"Does it mean anything, Maman, bread and milk and soap?"

"Kindness, I suppose. God knows, that's in short supply," Maman said. She tucked the anonymous treasure into her handbag.

"Who sent them?" Natalie asked.

Maman shrugged.

Natalie had a headache. She went to bed to get warm, thinking about kindness coupons.

Someone must invent them. Kindness coupons to trade for crusty baguettes spread with butter and cheese, like Brie from Normandy or chicken liver paté. Or better still, coupon gifts for *Coq au Vin*, Swiss Ovaltine, oranges, beef stew with bay leaves and thyme, rice pudding and cherry jam. The kindness coupons could bring warmer weather to go shopping any time or to plant flowers in the garden again. The gifts could be used for new wallpaper or coal and anthracite, loads and loads of it, to heat the damp house. She hoped to receive a flood of kindness coupons she could trade for new mattresses, for erasing all badges with the Star of David, and sleeping without nightmares. Her imagination filled with coupon dreams for visiting Pierre in Switzerland, bringing Rose back from England, and for Lilla to remember Papa and for her to go on botany hikes with him. Yes, kindess coupons could be invented and used for medical school, for freeing prisoners—for raising the dead.

Chapter 45

Boys

Since winter, Natalie had accumulated problems. It hardly seemed fair with her working so hard at solutions. It started with her friend Caroline's birthday party. Maman dared not accompany Natalie, so Hélène went with her to the villa behind gray walls covered in ivy on Rue du Cours Albert.

Caroline had a seventeen-year-old brother named Eric. As they played musical chairs, he accidentally pushed Natalie, who fell on the carpet. Caroline decreed that Eric must kiss her. A hush fell over the girls.

Eric was gangly with yellow hair and pimples on his face. Natalie felt her face grow hot as Eric bent down toward her. A first kiss was supposed to be exciting, but all she got was a peck on the cheek. She felt humiliated and cheated.

Soon the girls were chattering again, eating black-market vanilla cake. Eric left to play tennis. Caroline rushed Natalie to the bathroom, saying Eric had a crush on her, and asking her what it felt like to kiss, and did she love him? Natalie, blushing, was saved by Hélène's arrival.

"I have a good mind to tell your mother about your kissing games," Hélène told Caroline.

Caroline brought her hands over her mouth. If Papa were home, Natalie would rush to him and tell him. He would know what she should say and what she should do. She had no one to help her.

That night Natalie realized that boys were a major problem and, apart from Eric, she didn't know any. She must find out about them. She went to the library and checked books out. "Natalie is a bookworm," Maman said to someone on the phone. Natalie tried to imagine what Papa would say, but she could not. She was almost thirteen and she ought to know about boys. One day, she hoped she would get married—unless the German killed all the men and the boys.

In the stories she read, the boys were always smiling, strong and steady as tree trunks, and the girls were weak and caused all the problems. After a stupid quarrel, the boy married his girlfriend. The boy and his girl prayed together aloud. That was silly.

Then there were the cheap novels in the attic, left behind by some maid. They were awful, but a change from Nazi atrocities. The romance covers depicted clothes ripped open in passion and women with bare breasts. The girl lay with her chin up as if she wanted her throat slit. Was that what people did? Natalie tried to imagine what Maman would say if she or Hélène came home with torn clothes after a party.

What a man and a woman did in bed was so inconceivable that Natalie decided it was a minor problem. Still, what could the descriptions mean: "ecstasy burnt their entwined flesh," "she gave herself totally," or "their flesh was one?"

Even if Papa were home, Natalie wasn't sure she could have talked about it with him. She tried to figure out what he would say, but all she remembered was his talk of maps. There were no maps to show the way to behave with a man.

Would a strong man want her, with her skinny arms and tiny breasts? They were growing, but slowly. They were the size of small lemons, and there was something wrong with them because when she touched her nipples, they tingled. How could it possibly feel good when a man touched your breasts?

Lips were a problem as well. Natalie read about them. Sometimes she prayed, arguing with herself that if God existed, he would grant her voluptuous lips. Voluptuous was a fascinating word. It made her feel dreamy. A man might overlook her small breasts if he wanted to kiss her badly enough. That would be one less problem. She was glad she'd thought of that. That must be what the girls called "sex."

After school, older girls in the cloakroom often discussed boys. Natalie usually found the topic disgusting and walked away, but today, she listened. A girl said that boys had a long tube between their legs. The tube shot tadpoles inside you. It made you bleed, but it also made you bleed often after that, for no reason. The bleeding caused pain and that made you a woman. Otherwise you were an old maid. If it was true, it didn't seem worth it. But in order not to be an old maid, she would have to be wounded by the tube. That was a serious problem. Not one she could raise with Maman. Maybe not even with Hélène.

Food was a more urgent problem. It had been seventeen days since they'd eaten potatoes. Hélène kept count. The only milk the dairy sold was sour. Maman told Hélène to bring the sour milk home next time. She'd read that she could use it to make fritters, with or without apples, or fat, or eggs. Natalie remained worried about sex. It sound disgusting.

Chapter 46

Potato Harvest

Around the meandering Seine, half an hour away on foot, the potato harvest was in progress. The entire crop was requisitioned by the Wehrmacht, whose gray-green trucks were filled with heaps of potatoes. The largest were long gone by sundown. Only older people worked the furrows, entitled by custom to take home the tiny, leftover potatoes.

From the nebulous darkness, Natalie watched the last old man leave. Then she moved into a furrow. Squeezing soil between her fingers, she filled her net bag with potatoes smaller than eggs. She scraped her wood-soled shoes on a rock by the edge of the last furrow and walked along unlit streets, reaching home without a problem after curfew. Maman was delighted with Natalie's harvest.

The following day, Natalie tried to repeat her exploit. She reached home indignant, with only five small potatoes at the bottom of her bag. Her cheeks and arms were grazed and her legs bruised. Angry old folks had pelted her with stones. She couldn't go back to the fields, although it was now her mission to provide food since Maman trusted her to get provisions.

At night, she dreamt she'd stolen veal chops and raspberry jam from the Germans, hiding them inside her schoolbag. Yet, when she reached home, she found her schoolbag empty and only an alarm clock ticking inside Maman's bicycle basket. She woke up drenched in perspiration. During the day, she forgot her nightmares, but in the evening, she went to bed as late as possible, afraid of what the dark would bring.

Chapter 47

Parachute

Maman melted stumps of candles to make new ones, so they'd have light during power failures. She peered over the bowl of wax, where she was about to dip a string wick. Without looking up, she said, "I want you to try shopping again, Natalie. You manage pretty well."

Natalie was buoyed by the praise and hoped for more. It was too early for the shops to open, so Natalie took off to see Béret, an odd, gruff old man on crutches without a family who'd appeared a few years ago. He lived near the Seine, in a dilapidated shack far from neighbors, on an unpaved path the Germans didn't bother to explore. From time to time, he sold radishes, cabbages, or turnips from his plot. His customers were housewives on endless quests for food.

With the vitamin cookies saved in her pocket at school recess, Natalie was hopping over the pot-holed county road leading to the path when great banging from German Defense guns mounted on the roof of the town hall shot at specks of foreign planes high in the sky. Natalie knew that when the parachutes opened, the Americans in their harnesses were in danger. To prevent them from landing alive, the Germans on the ground had orders to shoot them in the face. She was glad never to have witnessed such a sight. She heard that some parachutes had landed at night, and were long gone when the Germans hunted the neighborhood for them.

Sitting on weeds, hands above her eyes, she scrutinized the sky. The hammering went on for minutes before an eerie quiet settled in. Then, like a giant anemone with its petals open, all unfurled, a parachute floated down. It fell sideways in a fallow field a few yards away.

Natalie ran toward the man who pulled at the parachute like a fisherman hauling in a net full of fish. The soldier in the strange uniform freed himself from straps and ropes around his shoulders and hips and leaned sideways, before falling on his side. He sat on the ground, rubbing his face. Natalie stood in front of him in her old gingham dress, next to his collapsing, oversized balloon, offering him the last of her vitamin cookies. He didn't see her. She put her cookies in his hand, bending his large fingers over it.

The man blinked as if he'd just woken up. "Lo?" he asked.

Water? Natalie gestured to indicate that she was going for help. The man frowned. Natalie picked up a pointy rock and drew a house on the ground, with an arrow going toward it. Without getting up, the airman pointed to Beret's roof.

Natalie nodded several times to mean "Yes, yes!" Then she ran to tell Béret.

Béret was in an especially bad mood. "I'll attend to him," he shouted, "I knew he was coming, see?" When Natalie didn't answer, he added, "My cousin!" He grabbed her by the shoulders, his nose close to her face. "My cousin, yes! If you tell a single earthly soul, I'll kill you. Hear? Now get out of my way!" Mad Béret shot past her, his crutches forgotten by the door, his crippled legs intact.

Chapter 48

Allied Landing

1944 had started as usual with plenty of new restrictions and bad news.

Now it was spring. Natalie reached the grocery store on foot. Instead of the usual forlorn line of housewives and old men waiting their turn to buy turnips or gray macaroni, she found everybody speaking at the same time, laughing. She waited to be served. People all discussed the Allied landing in Normandy. Since no one approached the grocer's cash register, she moved to the counter.

"Quickly, you'll have good news to take home for a change," the grocer said.

Natalie didn't know who he was talking to. She said, "I need sugar, please, if you have any. And a box of matches." She held out her coupon books.

The grocer didn't pay attention. He was engrossed in conversation with several people at once, waving his arms, shaking his hands, twirling as if he were drunk. Perhaps he was. In other circumstances, Natalie would have been alarmed, but the crowd was also in high spirits, sharing details of an American landing.

When the grocer looked down, he re-discovered her. "Ah! You have to make allowances today of all days! It's not often that people come here and go home with bags full of good news! Go home, tell your mother it's confirmed! Solid! Written in stone!"

"I need a box of matches, and three sugar rations for J3 category," Natalie insisted.

"Good," he said, dropping three boxes of matches and a whole box of sugar cubes into her net bag although the coupons entitled her only to a third of a box. "Pay if you like."

Shopping without paying was unheard of, so Natalie put money on the counter. The grocer dropped a handful of change back into her hand without counting, and clapped his hands over his head, stamping his feet, cheering with clients. Natalie counted the coins.

"Monsieur," she said, "that's too much money."

"Well, who cares? Take it and run. Spread the news."

Natalie stood for a bit, listening to make sure the Normandy Allied landing was confirmed. Then she ran all the way home with her net shopping bag banging against her legs.

"Maman," she shouted as she opened the door, "Listen, they're coming! It's true, the grocer says so. Lots of people have seen them."

"What? Americans? What are you talking about?"

"In Normandy! The Germans are all going back to Germany. American tanks are coming, wave after wave of them, and people are kissing them!" She blurted out her news in such a confusing way that Maman had to piece together for herself the unbelievable news that American troops were racing from Normandy's beaches toward Paris.

"Wonderful!" Hélène hooted. She ran upstairs and slid down the banister several times, which was forbidden, singing "The Marseillaise" off-key, while Lilla clapped her hands in the hallway.

"How can we be sure the Americans have landed? We heard rumors before."

"It's really, really true!" Natalie insisted, dizzy with the good news. "People have seen the tanks, thousands of tanks. Everybody says so. It's true! You'll see."

Maman tore two of her oldest white bedsheets into strips and dipped them into buckets filled with blue or red ink mixed with boiling water. In the bathroom, the flag fabric dripped all night into the bathtub. In the morning, Maman spread them to dry on a line at the back of the house.

"How many points to an American star, Natalie?' she asked in the morning. "You don't know? Why not? What do they teach you at school? Run upstairs, ask Hélène. Hurry, I don't have all day."

Instead of the typewriter, the Singer sewing machine was enthroned on the table, to create friendly flags.

Chapter 49

Sour Bread

Two days later, before she and Hélène could tie Maman's new flags to the balconies, their worst nightmare took place. The Germans came back. Only this time, it was four white-haired German officers in black Luftwaffe uniforms, shepherding adolescent boys, who flung open the garden gate and set up camp in the garden.

A white-haired, wrinkled officer politely asked Natalie to plug their electric food cart extension inside the house. Maman grabbed her shawl with the Star of David from the banister, and didn't dare set foot outside. Her damp flags waited, rolled around the mop handle, deep inside the broom cupboard.

The young German soldiers had voices like girls. They had no hair on their faces and never smiled. Hélène refused to go out, even in the garden. The arrival of this latest contingent of Germans transformed her into Madame Jeune Sorpa—*Je ne sors pas*—I don't go out.

The officers, who sometimes sat on the front steps, showed Lilla photos of their children and grandchildren, while the young recruits stared at them with gleaming eyes, colder than marbles, their hands on their guns.

The German officer in the haughty visor and silver decorations often visited Natalie in her nightmares, threatening to throw bombs on the roof. Natalie woke up just as the house was about to explode.

Waking up in the dark on the seventh morning of the garden's invasion, Natalie heard scratchy sounds coming from the garden. She tiptoed into Hélène's room and shook her awake. In their nightdresses, the sisters opened the shutters just enough to peer below.

The garden gate was open. Limping or fit, young or old, each German soldier cut branches and twigs from the lilacs, the mock orange blossom, the oak, even the boxwood. Oblivious to ridicule, each fastened the branches to the net on his helmet as camouflage before slipping away.

Then they were gone, and no more came. Baffling noises like distant explosions boomed in the distance for hours, followed, during brief intermissions, by the howling of dogs. At home, all was quiet, except for the ringing of the phone. Someone told Maman that their area, in a loop of the Seine, was still guarded by the latest units of the German Luftwaffe. Some bridges over the Seine, mined by departing Germans units, had exploded.

Natalie dressed fast and ran into the stripped garden. Though it was spring, the lawn's central maple, as well as most of the huge oak over the garage, had reverted to winter outlines. One of the ropes of the swing had been cut so that it hung off balance.

Beneath the dining room window where the Germans' electric cart had stood, Natalie spotted a lump of something sitting on a burlap bag. She picked it up and inspected it. Bread speckled with orange mold. A whole loaf! Enough for four slices each, it would be a good breakfast, after scraping off the rotten parts. Natalie found the burlap bag that the bread had rested on half-filled with roasted coffee beans. Carrying her treasures, she ran indoors.

"Look what I found, Maman! Lots of coffee beans." She waited for exclamations of delight.

Maman wore her bluish-black hair in four parallel rolls on top of her head. Curly wisps fell over her neck. Without speaking, she leaned over Natalie's find, sliding her hands under the beans with an odd expression—one that Natalie had seen on train passengers waking up in strange places. Maman was about to share a precious secret or a memory with her.

Natalie wanted to throw her arms around her. But Hélène chose the moment to burst into the room with a clatter. Maman's confidential expression vanished.

Clasping her hands behind her, Maman said, as if she knew that their good life could never return, "That's not coffee, my dear. Only toasted acorns."

The beautiful moment had passed without a shared joy. Head lowered, Natalie carried the disgraceful bag across the lawn. She threw it into the latrines the Germans had dug behind the shrubs in the farthest corner of the garden. Angry, she kicked lumps of clay over the acorns before returning indoors.

In the kitchen, Hélène, looking grown-up at almost seventeen with a smear of red lipstick, busily scraped off orange spots from the dark loaf of bread. She cut two slices with the serrated knife. Lilla, craning her neck, wrinkled her nose and left. Hurrying, before the unreliable electricity went off again, Natalie and Hélène each inserted a slice of the German bread into the toaster.

The bread was very sour.

Chapter 50

Pontoons

The newspapers were filled with news of the Allied advance. Nothing seemed to hamper the Americans. Where old stone bridges had been blown off, they built floating ones, called pontoons, which French people had never seen. Because of the miracle of pontoons, which carried troops, material and emergency vehicles, Le Vésinet was liberated at the same time as Paris. Everybody was excited, laughing, hugging, and singing.

Natalie wished she could be like the Americans, who had good ideas and managed to produce new things fast. She wanted to go out and explore the neighborhood, and perhaps get new ideas, but Maman, afraid of another reversal, kept her girls from school and stayed indoors with them. The Americans were still far away in Normandy.

Monsieur Jean Veupat—I don't want any—and Madame Tropafaire—too much to do—no longer came to call. Frau Maufaitan—foul weather—may have died during the bombings. It served her right for being a Nazi, the sisters agreed.

"Are all the Germans nasty, even the children?" Lilla asked at breakfast.

Maybe not, but who wanted to think about them when celebration was everywhere? Natalie was thinking of the excitement of the parades, with French, Americans, and Canadians, the tanks decked in flowers, and songs, kisses, and dancing in the streets!

Maman had new guests. Sometimes she smiled. The handsome Harry Cover—*haricot vert*, green bean—whose name was pronounced with a British accent, came with his best friend John Duff—*Jaune d'oeuf*—egg yolk.

Hélène said, "I'm almost seventeen. I'm too old to play dress up. That's for kids."

"Who says you are a grown-up? Not me," Natalie grumbled.

Twenty minutes later, a young man in a musty tuxedo with a yellowed shirt and black bow tie rang the doorbell.

"Call me Marchais, *Marché Noir,* Mr. Black Market told his sisters in a phony deep voice. "Film actor-director-producer. I can produce anything you need. For a price, of course."

Harry Cover did his best to shoo him away. Marchais Noir left, but Hélène, as his girlfriend Ellie Coptaire, *helicoptere*, brought news of his exploits.

Gradually these visitors vanished too, as did the old dress-up clothes from the moleskin trunk, mildewed and frayed, handed over to the ragman when Maman succumbed to an attack of house cleaning. She justified this by saying that she soon hoped to find a job as a secretary for one of the new papers sprouting all over France since the Allied landing.

Chapter 51

A Perm

After the Allied landing on June 14, 1944, there were bombings during their advance, when pupils were taken down into underground tunnels where, before the war, green bananas from Africa were spread on the ground to ripen. Deep underground, the electricity worked even more erratically. There were no blackboards in the tunnels so the classes were interrupted. Later, there was much catching up to do. Two weeks were added to the school year, but that had ended on July 1.

Now it was August and the allies were moving north to liberate Paris. Everybody was planning celebrations and making ready for the allies. There would be masses of Allied flags fluttering from rooftops and windows, a mayoral speech, and a great parade with the Free Forces of the Interior—FFI for short. Resistance people and their leaders with armbands would be there, and tanks from the American, British and Canadian Forces along with drums and military music. "The Marseillaise" was to be sung by a chorus of children along the parade route dressed in red, white, and blue. The newspapers announced that fireworks with rockets would light up the sky all night. Everyone would dance in the streets to the sound of violins and concertinas. Picnic lunches and dinners were planned in the parks, which Jews at long last could enjoy like everyone else.

Hélène, who would soon be seventeen, had cajoled Maman for weeks, begging for a perm for the occasion. Maman had relented. Hélène wasted no time in making an appointment with the local hairdresser. Timidly, Natalie told Maman that she, too, would like a change of hairstyle, hoping for a shorter haircut. Maman said, "Maybe later. I can't afford it now."

As if restrictions for the Jews were still in effect, Maman, who no longer needed to sign her name daily at the police station, rarely left home. She told Natalie to accompany Hélène to the hair appointment.

It felt good to walk in the sunshine without fear as if the memories of the German occupation and the harsh winters were dissipating. Tall Hélène looked like a queen with a turbaned towel over her washed, damp hair. Since hairdressers had no shampoo or towels, clients provided their own. In Paris, young men pedaled for hours in the basement of elegant beauty shops to produce the electricity needed upstairs to operate the dryers.

In Le Vésinet, no young athlete pedaled in the basement of the beauty shop squeezed between the grocer's and the blue hardware store. There were only four seats along faded pink walls with old mirrors marred by age spots. The owner and her assistants sat the women customers on an outside bench in the sun till it was time to remove their curlers.

Natalie sat, wrinkling her nose at the smell of hot irons and perm chemicals, both flattered and resentful as the hairdressers insisted she'd look better with shorter hair. They pinched strands of her curly black hair between two fingers as if they were scissors, head to one side, repeating, "Oh, you'd look so cute like this!"

The women gossiped about some scandal, but Natalie didn't pay attention. She wanted to forget the war. She tried to see how her own life could improve from now on, though Papa, Rosie, Grand-Papa, Pierre the gardener, and Maman's mother and father were missing. No one bothered to ask her how she felt. She took a book out of her pocket and read.

Hélène appeared in front of her, grinning, gorgeous, her blond hair waved and curled, patting her head and spinning for Natalie to admire her new hairstyle from all angles.

"Now we both have curly hair," Hélène said, taking her arm as they walked out. "Do you like me like this? I do!"

Elegant, grown-up Hélène paused to see her reflection in the shop window behind the seated women waiting their turn, caressing the bouncy curls above her ears. The sisters walked each other out into the sun. Suddenly Hélène ran back into the beauty shop. She'd forgotten Maman's towel on her chair. She smiled again at her reflection in the window, waiting for Natalie. It was fun to stand, arm in arm, and see themselves, one blond and one dark-haired, in the glass.

"From now on, we'll enjoy ourselves," Hélène said.

Yes, the Germans are gone. At least, we are free of their nastiness, Natalie thought. Everything would be different, more like life before the war. She hoped her nightmares would cease. She wanted to believe only good things would happen.

Before they had time to cross the street, unusual muffled sounds reached them from the direction of the marketplace.

Hélène stopped in her tracks. "A new parade. Let's go!"

"Maman will be angry if we're late," Natalie cautioned.

"Go home then and miss the fun. I'm going." She flew down the road with Natalie in pursuit.

A few minutes wouldn't delay them much. As they

turned right from the Rue des Ecoles into the Avenue Victor Hugo the sound swelled to raucous shouts. Without musicians or flags, a jagged procession rounded the corner.

From the sidewalk, Monsieur Henri, the grocer who had told Natalie about the American landing, goaded them. "Hey, Jewish girls, want a chance to get even?"

What was he talking about? Among the approaching crowd, Natalie recognized the postman in his shabby uniform. He shouted along with others taking gulps from wine bottles passed from hand to hand. Then Natalie saw the hairless woman at the head of the procession, bent over a lump in her arms. A man laughed as he poked her behind the knees with a bristle broom.

"Hop, hop! Show how you dance!" he screeched.

The crowd drew closer. It was a baby the hairless woman carried, its round head showing above a small blanket. The woman's face was white. Her eyes were wide. Her lower lip was swollen. It bled onto her chin.

Behind the woman with the baby marched the pharmacist and the private piano teacher who lived across the street, walking arm in arm with the knife sharpener and mean old Béret, who'd threatened to kill her when she'd asked his help for the airman with the parachute. Behind them came the woman who mopped the canteen floor after lunch. Fists punching the air, they all gesticulated, their faces distorted.

"Come on, girls! Join Yolande's party," Madame Coiret, the pharmacist's wife, called.

Yolande? The only Yolande in the neighborhood was the Mercinars' pretty maid. The woman with a bare skull, who looked like a doll with torn-off hair, was the Mercinars' maid. She stumbled more than she walked. Her left sleeve was ripped at the shoulder. Only her legs moved as she progressed in the middle of the street unblinking, carrying the baby.

"What happened to her?" Natalie asked. "She planted a stinking German flower in her stinking flowerpot! Like stinking Josiane, the shoe repairman's girl, that's what," the baker said, cursing, hands on his hips.

The crowd was now in front of the sisters. People picked up garbage and threw it at Yolande.

"It's not for you to punish this girl," a familiar voice shouted. "We have courts in this country."

Mademoiselle Leblanc, the elementary school principal, stood in the street in front of the crowd, the way she stood in school in front of her blackboard.

"Who needs the courts? She done wrong, and we've had it," people shouted.

"Have you taken leave of your senses? It's the German father who needs to be punished. Our enemy," Mademoiselle shouted. "There's a child's life to consider."

"You defend a woman who slept with the Krauts?" a red-faced man sneered, getting closer.

"I don't see you going after the rich women in town who did the same, or worse," Mademoiselle retorted, standing her ground.

Mademoiselle was right, but in the street, nobody listened. People went on pelting Yolande with garbage. Children threw pebbles at her. A dog barked right behind her. Someone hit Yolande on the side of the head with a mud ball that splattered on her exposed shoulder. Suddenly, mud dripped onto Hélène's dress. Hélène drew back and tried to mop up the stain with her towel.

A man shouted, "Good shot. Again! Do it again! Who's next?"

"You two with us or against?" Madame Coiret asked, reaching for Hélène's elbow.

Natalie pulled Hélène away as Madame Coiret's husband barked, "Leave the Jewish kids out of it, Jeanine."

Slipping and pushing between jeering people, Natalie and Hélène made their way to the opposite sidewalk and ran off.

"Why are they mad at Yolande?" Natalie asked.

"She slept with the Germans."

"Perhaps she only slept with one. Perhaps she didn't even sleep with one. Perhaps it's not her baby. She's only a maid. They should have asked the Mercinars."

"The Mercinars left weeks ago for Germany with Georgette, taking dozens of suitcases. Yolande was left to take care of the house."

"How do you know?"

"Everyone at the beauty shop talked about it," Hélène said. "You were there, you heard it."

Natalie said, "No. I didn't. I was reading. What did they say?"

"This morning, someone found her lover hiding in the Mercinars' basement. There was enough canned food down there to last them for months, they said. Imagine, tins of sardines, sacks of potatoes, jars of honey, and three hams! Yolande cooked with real white flour and olive oil. Do you remember olive oil? No? I don't either. I bet it's good though. The man pretended he wasn't German, but he couldn't speak a word of French."

"How did they speak to each other, then?"

"How should I know? She must have picked up enough German during the Mercinars parties. Remember the Hotchkiss cars parked in front of their house most of the time."

"Why did the German soldier stay behind?"

"His officers told him to wait for them to return with reinforcements. He was wounded, in the shoulder, I think.

Yolande said he stayed because of the baby, so that means he's the father."

Natalie said, "But surely they love each other. When they get married, the baby will have a Papa. That's good, isn't it?"

Hélène shrugged. "The FFI, the Resistance men, took him away. To shoot him, I think. Everybody says Yolande is a disgrace, because, at eighteen, a girl should know better."

Eighteen! Only a year older than Hélène. They walked in silence.

Once home, Natalie hid in her room, shaking. "Poor, poor Yolande," she murmured, wishing Yolande knew how she felt. That night, the German officer she may have killed came to her in a dream and ordered her to hide him in the basement, behind moldy trunks, folding chairs, and the broken old garage doors.

Awake early the next morning, freed from the threats of the German officer during the day, Natalie found the world a sad place. The Germans were no longer around, true, but that was all. Nothing was repaired. Nothing had returned to the way it was before the war. The Germans were beastly, but the French people, whom she so far believed to be good, were unfair and very cruel, too.

1945

Chapter 52

The Motorcycle

Waking up one Sunday morning, still hearing the guttural accent of the German officer in his black uniform who had threatened to shoot her if she refused to open the garage door, Natalie stumbled into the bathroom. As she wet the corner of her towel to wash her face, she realized she'd had another nightmare. The Germans were gone.

She brushed her teeth with baking soda since even when handing in an empty tube at the pharmacy as required, there was no toothpaste to be had. She combed her hair. As she tied her braids, she heard a frightening rumble. From the window, she saw a large black motorcycle roaring in through the gate. The bulky man riding it left it against the hedge and knocked hard on the front door. Natalie went downstairs, heart pounding so hard, she had to hold on to the banister or she would have fallen down.

Maman had already opened the door. "Monsieur?"

"No. Not Monsieur," he repeated. "Come on, Noémi, don't you recognize me? I'm Jacob, your brother."

Maman took a step back, hitting her chest with her fist. "What are you saying?"

"I'll take off my helmet." He did. "Do you know me now?"

Maman uttered a strangling noise before throwing herself at the stranger. "I thought...I was afraid you were—"

she stammered. She clung to him as they went into the sitting room.

"What are you doing in an American uniform? Do you work for them?"

"It's a British uniform. I work as a translator. I'm on loan to the Americans for the time being. But tell me about you, Noémi," he said.

Maman noticed Natalie at the door. "This is Natalie. She'll be fourteen in August." To Natalie, eyes shining, she said, "This is your Oncle Jacob, my brother. Do you remember him?" Holding on to him, she added, "Give him a kiss."

Natalie hesitated to kiss the stranger. She offered him her hand.

"A good enough start," Oncle Jacob laughed, sitting down in Papa's studded leather armchair.

Maman should have pointed to another seat, Natalie thought. That was a special chair.

"Make us some tea, Natalie," Maman said, "then wake up your sisters." Turning to the dark-haired stranger, she added, "I'm sorry we have little to offer."

Oncle Jacob leaned on his right knee to fish out things from his rear left pocket.

He announced, "I have everything for a decent breakfast right here, and here, and here." He emptied his front pants pockets, then his rear pockets, then his leather jacket pockets till the coffee table was covered with packets and tins, tubes and boxes.

Maman and Natalie held their breath.

"Is this for us? All of it?" Natalie asked, facing the profusion of goods.

"No one here but family, and we all want breakfast, right?" He laughed again. "Tuna fish, K-rations, chocolate, condensed milk, coffee powder, cookies, and crackers."

"Why did you say, 'coffee powder'?" Natalie asked. She also wondered about the K-rations that came in what looked like tuna fish cans.

"You've not heard of coffee powder? That's what American troops are given. I'd never heard of it before the war either. It's pretty good." Oncle Jacob tore open a little foil packet. "Here, smell it."

Natalie bent over it. The powder had a pleasant smell. "Give it to Maman," she murmured, remembering with shame the sack of toasted acorns she'd brought in, thinking Maman would be happy to have coffee beans again.

"It's all hers!" Oncle Jacob said, laughing again. He laughed a lot.

Natalie made and brought in the chamomile tea, and went to sit on the last step of the stairs, elbows on her knees, to listen to the conversation between Maman and her brother, since the door was open. She had not heard anything about him or anyone of Maman's family since the war started.

"What about your in-laws? Do they help you?" he asked.

"It's rather the other way around." Maman told him about Pauline hiding in the garage, and how she took Pauline to her Swiss friends.

"What happened to Marc after his arrest?"

Her hands clenched, Maman spoke fast. "He was released after three days, as I told Pauline he would be. But Jacob, I don't want to talk about them. Tell me, do you have news of our family?"

Oncle Jacob told Maman that their parents had been arrested in 1942, and that seven members of their extended family, whose names Natalie didn't catch, had died in German camps. In the growing silence, Maman asked about Miriam.

Oncle Jacob said, "She's alive."

"Alive?" Maman asked in a low voice. "What do you mean, alive? Where is she?"

"In the camp, she tried to rip the number off her arm," Oncle Jacob said. "They beat her so hard, she lost her mind. When I found out she'd been liberated, I went to see her on one of my leaves. I had her transferred to a private clinic in Chantilly."

"Do you mean, you pay for Miriam's care?"

"The government pays, but not enough. I visit her from time to time, but she sometimes gets upset when she sees me."

"Isn't there hope? Some treatment?"

"Her doctors believe the damage was severe enough to be permanent. She believes she's in a rest home for a few weeks."

"Did you tell her that's not the case?"

"I don't have the heart to take her only comfort away, Noémi."

Natalie was aghast. Oncle Jacob, whom she liked because he put them in a good mood, knew horrible things about Maman's family. He was good. She wished she had kissed him. But all the same, how could he laugh so much, knowing what he knew?

Upstairs she found Lilla barefoot in her robe, her unbrushed hair over her face, moaning about wanting Maman. Natalie found Lilla's slippers under the bed, knelt to help her put them on, and sent her downstairs before clattering along to Hélène's room.

"There is a man talking to Maman! Our uncle Jacob. I saw him arrive on a motorcycle. He wears a British uniform. He brought lots of food packets for breakfast. Are you listening, Hélène? Hurry up. Maman wants you downstairs."

As long as she spoke, Natalie could ignore what had happened to Maman's mother and father or their aunts and uncles.

Oncle Jacob came four more times, leaving after dinner on his noisy motorcycle for his military base. He always brought food and promised to return. He sat at the head of the table like Papa. Natalie didn't like it at first, but he made Maman laugh, and they were all in such a good mood that she accepted it. When Maman asked Oncle Jacob where he intended to settle after the war, he told them that he would go back to England, where he lived with his wife, Muriel, in Liverpool.

"You married an English woman!" Maman exclaimed, as if he'd married a Nazi.

Oncle Jacob explained that he had a job lined up with the Phillips Company that manufactured radios and gramophones. He made it sound as if Liverpool was as close as the next town. But Natalie knew there was an ocean between them, and miles of country and water separating them.

There was also much money to be saved to buy a train ticket, then a ferryboat ticket to reach England, and another train ticket to Liverpool, even if you made a plan and took a map with you.

Chapter 53

A Riddle

Maman's typewriter had been put away. It was a Sunday. Oncle Jacob was coming to lunch. He appeared as usual on his purring, puttering, groaning motorcycle, carrying a large khaki rucksack, which he kept between his feet as he sat down at table. He'd handed Maman many packages when he arrived. She was busy in the kitchen. Natalie liked the table set with an ironed tablecloth, which hid the cracks in the yellow oilcloth. There was a posy of pink clover and tiny daisies from the garden in the middle.

Oncle Jacob sat at Papa's place without being told to.

"I have a riddle for you girls. Here is the riddle. Can you guess why I'm so proud of your mother?"

No one answered till Lilla offered, "Because she had us?"

Once Jacob laughed and clapped. "That's not what I meant, but for your effort, you get this!" From his backpack, he ceremoniously extracted an orange, which he held high over the table before dropping it into Lilla's hands.

Natalie and Hélène oohed and aahed. Lilla, seated next to Hélène, handed the orange to her.

"You peel it. I don't know how."

Hélène, watched by her sisters, peeled the orange, scraping the cottony white pith away, separating the sections part of the way, so the orange looked like an opening flower.

"There," she said. "Take it, Lilla."

Lilla took a section and carried the orange to Natalie on the other side of the table. Natalie took a section before returning the magic fruit to Hélène.

"What's this? Don't you like oranges?" Oncle Jacob asked, frowning.

Lilla nodded. "We must always share. Maman says so."

"I see," he said. "Of course you must share. But not today. Today, you have that orange all to yourself!"

The scent of the orange peel was thrilling. So was its brightness on Hélène's plate. When she brought the remaining sections to Oncle Jacob, he waved her hand away, so Hélène placed two sections on the rim of Maman's plate, in spite of Oncle Jacob's comment. Then each sister had a second section. They ate each with relish, tongues and gums tingling with pleasure.

"Maman gets upset if one of us has it all, and the rest of us have nothing," Hélène explained.

"So to get a whole orange all to yourself, answer my question. Why am I so very proud of my sister?"

"Your little sister, "Lilla corrected.

"My little sister, yes, Lilla. Hélène, can you tell me?"

"Because she never said she was afraid?"

"Cold, Hélène. You're cold!" He raised his chin toward the other side of the table, where Natalie sat by herself. "Your turn. Any ideas?"

"Because...because she learned to type?"

"A bit warmer! Keep going!" He waved his hand in a come-on gesture.

"Because sometimes she went out without her Star of David?" Lilla burst out, lifting her elbows off the table.

"That was forbidden, wasn't it?" he said. "You're warmer. Why do you think she did?"

"Because she is a good student?" Hélène mimed holding a pencil and writing something.

"Depends what you mean."

"I mean, she practiced at home a lot." Hélène gave a sigh.

"She did. And she was always in a bad mood, when she did, even with me!" Liliane said. "She wouldn't let me play house under the table when she typed."

"Warmer, Lilla. Natalie and Hélène, help your little sister," Oncle Jacob urged, bending his fingers toward his palms.

Natalie searched her mind for the right answer. "Because she typed? "

"What did she type?" he insisted. "If you tell me, you win this orange." He pulled another splendid orange out of his rucksack and displayed it on his palm.

"I don't know," Natalie admitted. "But it must have been important. Lilla is right. Maman was always angry if we came in when she sat at the typewriter. We had to stay out of the dining room when she practiced."

Oncle Jacob rubbed his chin with one hand. "During the week, you went to school. Where do you think your Maman went?" He made circles with his hands.

"Sometimes she went out without her Star of David! I know, because her scarf was stuffed inside Papa's old rubber boot. Ask Natalie," Lilla said. "She found the scarf with the star inside a boot. Maman pulled it out when she came home and she laid it on the banister."

"Where did she go?"

"To her school in Paris?" Natalie asked.

Oncle Jacob said, "You understand, don't you, that without her star, Maman could not be singled out so easily."

"But if a neighbor denounced her for not wearing it, it

would have been terrible!" Natalie declared, biting her lower lip at the thought.

They fell silent while Maman brought in the water jug, then the salad bowl. "Lunch is almost ready." She walked out.

Oncle Jacob got up, opened the bottle of wine he'd brought, letting it make a popping sound, and he poured a little wine into the water already in the girls' water glasses, just enough to color the water pink.

"We'll toast your Maman as soon as you guess," he said. "So hurry up and tell me!"

Hélène sighed, crossing her arms. "I've no idea. I'm no good at guessing games."

"None of you guessed, I see," Oncle Jacob concluded. "That shows what a superior job she's done."

No!" Lilla corrected him, "Maman doesn't have a job. Jews aren't allowed."

"I didn't mean a paying job."

Natalie felt as if she were trying to see through a fog. "You mean, Maman did something on her typewriter that—" She couldn't finish her sentence, because a lump suddenly threatened to fill her throat.

Oncle Jacob nodded slowly, looking at her. "Warmer, much warmer. Keep going, Natalie."

"Maman typed something?"

"Hot. You're so hot, Natalie, you're almost burning," he said, keeping his hands up like a man asked to hold a baby.

Natalie felt dizzy. Nothing came to mind. She gave up. Never mind that she wouldn't get the glowing orange Oncle Jacob had carefully balanced on the rim of his water glass.

Maman came in, carrying a platter of meat she placed in front of Oncle Jacob. "Please slice the roast you brought us while I get the potatoes. Lilla, come along," she commanded. "You can carry the gravy boat for me."

There was silence at the table till they heard footsteps in the hall as Maman and Lilla had returned.

"Shall I tell your children what you did with your typewriter, Noémi?" Oncle Jacob asked Maman.

"Why don't we leave that alone," Maman proposed, "and enjoy our lunch instead?" She sat down, flipping her napkin open before spreading it on her lap.

Oncle Jacob didn't listen. He clapped his hands. "For your patience and for trying to guess my very hard riddle, you each get an orange. Maman does too."

The rucksack between Oncle Jacob's feet was filled with endless marvels. He threw an orange over the table into Natalie's, then into Hélène's raised hands.

The girls giggled and displayed their orange on the rim of their glasses as Oncle Jacob had done, while he placed Maman's orange on her glass.

"I'll tell you, girls. Your mother was sometimes kept busy translating and typing coded papers filled with information about the Germans. These she delivered in Paris to someone who transmitted the information to England by radio. England and America made good use of it. But you knew nothing of your mother's work for the French Resistance," he concluded, holding up his wine glass toward Maman.

"For the Resistance!" Natalie laughed and sobbed at the same time. "Maman! Oh! Maman, you're so brave!" She got up so fast that her chair bounced twice to the floor like shutters slammed open against a wall. She ran to Maman and hugged her.

"Oh, you are so very brave, Maman!"

Maman enclosed her in her arms. Natalie thought her heart was exploding inside her.

Chapter 54

Life Goes On

Several days went by, and ordinary life went on without fun. Oncle Jacob was gone. No one sat in Papa's chair or presided at the head of the table. No one made them laugh. Natalie, Hélène and Lilla closed doors gently, instead of slamming them, in a new quiet no longer required since Maman didn't translate or type reports anymore.

One evening Maman said, "Oncle Jacob phoned. He is about to be sent to Germany or Italy with other translators for the American troops. He wasn't sure where or when. I hope he comes back and surprises us again soon."

They missed him. Maman worried about him, Natalie could tell from the way she frowned and sighed when his name was mentioned.

Neighbors sometimes dropped in, and although Maman smiled as long as they stayed, they told war stories, and it didn't seem as if she enjoyed their visits.

After they left, Maman declared to her daughters that they had better things to do than read the newspapers. But Hélène sometimes managed to read some headlines and bits of articles before Maman burned them.

Hélène told Natalie, "The German troops are in full retreat, I read this morning. They are beaten now, but they try to resist in Italy and Holland."

In June, Hélène read news to Natalie from stories she'd cut out of two different papers. "The Allies are now streaming into Germany," she said when she finished.

There were so many new names and functions to learn. Natalie found it confusing. Dwight Eisenhower, Roosevelt and Harry Truman—the new President of the United States, didn't sound English or American. She tried to learn five new names every day. Bernard Montgomery, was he the same as Monty? Then there were Bradley, Patton, Jean de Lattre de Tassigny. There were Russian names too, but she'd heard little about Russia. Were the Russians Allies or enemies? What was so bad about the Communists who wanted to share everything? It was hard to figure out. Hélène might know.

In Hélène's room, bent over a map in the day's newspaper, Natalie discovered that Field Marshall Keitel had signed the surrender of the German Reich in the presence of Jean De Lattre de Tassigny, representing the French nation.

When she went shopping with either Hélène or Lilly, she found men and women gathered at cafes, gesticulating inside clouds of American and Gauloises cigarette smoke, fervently discussing the latest exploits of the Allies, all speaking at the same time with no one listening except her.

People were relieved that the Germans were beaten and gone. Yet for all the good news, life was grim. The remnants of war were everywhere, from the deep potholes in the streets to the bouquets of flowers at the foot of the walls where a plaque indicated that some young person had been shot there by the Nazis. The continuing restrictions and the standing skeleton of the house next door were constant reminders of what had been lost during the last six years.

They had no news of Oncle Jacob. Perhaps he, too, was lost. Natalie wondered whether the Louviers would come back and rebuild their exotic home, but they didn't return.

Families and teachers, priests, ministers and visitors to Natalie's school no longer admonished students to work hard and help at home because there was a war. Instead, every class was exhorted to work twice as hard to excel, not simply to make up for lost time, but to become leaders in their communities, because they were the bright future of the country.

There was little change in the routine. There were still half burned buildings, endless shortages, long lines at the shops, chores to be done, homework, and school to attend.

On the last Monday of June, Natalie sat in class, listening to her language teacher Mademoiselle LeBlanc, a strict grader, who had been her teacher the previous year. As she returned their latest compositions, she read portions of them aloud.

Mademoiselle read from Jacqueline's composition. "'Grandmother teaches me to make white lace with bobbins, You have to count all the time.'"

"Is that interesting, girls?" she asked.

No one commented.

"Good work, Jaqueline, but you need details," Mademoiselle said, "to make those bobbins clear to us."

She handed Jacqueline her notebook back. "What about this?" She read part of Sylvie's writing.

"I'll skip the paragraphs about the wife's disease," the teacher said. "'Maman often gives him food because he can't cook. He's a piano tuner. I asked him to come when Maman went to church to tune our piano. It took a long time, but he was done before she came home. She was very pleased.'"

"That's good," Raymonde shouted from the back. "Better than making lace!"

"Can you say why you like it?" Mademoiselle asked.

"It ends well," Raymonde yelled.

The class laughed. Raymonde beamed.

Moving around the classroom, the teacher returned most notebooks with or without comments, until only Natalie's composition remained in her hand. Natalie felt increasingly uncomfortable. Her hands became fists under her desk.

"Listen to this," Mademoiselle told the class, handing Natalie her work. "Stand up to read, Natalie. Start here." She pointed, returning to her desk on the front platform at the front of the room.

Natalie stood up, trembling, and read from the middle. "'Math is sometimes too hard, and for the French class, I can't always find the long words in the Larousse dic—'"

"Louder! We can't hear!" skinny Josette shouted from the back row.

Natalie started reading again, forcing herself to speak slowly, as if the girls were elsewhere, but loudly too. "'I ask Papa to help me. He always does. He tells me to go on when I want to stop, and to check my math twice for mistakes, and to remember my decimal points. He stays with me until I'm done, then I can go and play.'"

The class erupted. "What a liar! She made it up! She doesn't have a father!"

Natalie itched all over. Her secret was out and she sat down without being told. Papa *did* talk with her, but she knew she would pay dearly for having told the truth. The girls would make fun of her and, to make things worse, the teacher would punish her. Maman would be furious. She twisted her fingers for strength and patience and relief.

Jeanine, a girl at the front of the class stood up. "She lies! He died last year, her father did. She made it up, or she has visions," she turned to stick her tongue out at Natalie.

The teacher crossed her arms, always a bad sign.

"She can't have visions," red-haired Marie-Christine

pronounced, nose in the air, "She's not a Catholic. The Jews killed Jesus, so why would God speak to them? Jews can't have visions."

"Maybe she's 'lucinating," Ginette giggled, nudging Anne with an elbow.

Sonia, wiping the blackboard, turned around. "No, silly, she's not having visions."

Fernande interrupted. "Liars will be punished. She'll get punished all right."

Behind Natalie, Simone hissed, "It's a mortal sin to lie. You'll roast in hell."

Things were getting worse. They had been getting worse for a long time. What was the use of telling the truth if no one ever believed her? She hoped for the bell when she could run away from all the hateful girls.

Fernande went on, "Everybody knows her dad is dead! How can he talk to her? She's sick in the head, and that is that." She made a curling motion by her ear—send her to *Charenton l'hôpital des toqués,* the sick-in-the-head hospital!"

Mademoiselle stepped into the hallway where someone who had knocked handed her a small pile of books. Taking advantage of her absence, Jacqueline, always best in every subject, raised up from the front row. "Don't you understand anything? Natalie is only saying—"

Fernande didn't let her finish. "I bet Natalie lies in every class! Now no one will believe her."

"Natalie's my friend. Leave her alone!" Jacqueline shouted.

Natalie blinked her disbelief. Her friend? She had a friend at the school? How was it possible?

Mademoiselle was back. She snatched Natalie's notebook back, strode to the platform, and slapped it shut on her desk. She glared. "Silence!" she shouted. The girls were quiet. "Come and speak to me after class, Natalie," she instructed. With only a week of school left before the summer vacation, the last bell of the day shrilled.

The girls threw books, notebooks and fountain pens into their bags before lining up by their desks to file out.

Simone leaned toward Natalie. "Don't get ideas, Jew girl. I'll tell Father Martinot. He'll remind Jacqueline it was the Jews who killed Jesus. He listens to me."

Natalie looked down. She took her time packing her books and pencil box, waiting for all the girls to be gone. Then she approached the teacher. Mademoiselle opened Natalie's notebook again and pressed her thumb along the central fold to keep it open. Natalie saw two red circles around misspelled words on her first page. It was so bad that she'd not been given a grade. Would she get a zero and be sent home in disgrace?

Mademoiselle asked, "Does your father live at home, or does he only come to visit?"

Natalie hugged her school bag. "He doesn't," she murmured, concentrating on a broken blue chalk at her feet.

"Yet, you wrote that your father helps you when you ask."

Natalie nodded several times.

The teacher frowned. "Your classmates say that your father died."

Natalie's face was on fire. "In Switzerland, last year. He was very sick. I went over the mountains with my aunt to see him," she said between her teeth.

"Does anyone else come and speak to you that other people can't see?"

"No," Natalie said, puzzled. "Nobody."

"I see." Mademoiselle said after a pause, "Are you sure your Papa's presence isn't a dream?"

Natalie replied, "I'm not a boarder; boarders sleep at

the dormitory of the Lycée. I sleep at home, so I can't dream here."

"Yet, you see your father?"

"No," Natalie said with a dry throat. "I don't see him. He's behind me."

"How do you know it's your father?"

"He smooths my hair with his hand, and rests it on my shoulder. There," she pointed to the spot.

"And he speaks to you?"

"Yes. That is how he helps. "

"I see. What does he say?"

"He says things are hard at first, that I must practice more. I must persevere." It was the truth, yet when Natalie raised her eyes, the classroom was blurry.

Mademoiselle kept saying, "I see. I see." She took out her fountain pen and wrote something on the corner of Natalie's composition. Natalie didn't dare to look.

With one hand, Mademoiselle raised Natalie's chin and looked into her eyes.

"Take this composition to your mother, Natalie. Show her your grade. Have her sign your notebook and return it to me on Monday. Your mother will be very proud of you. Now I have a teachers' meeting to attend, and it's time for you to run home."

Natalie dared to glance at the corner of her composition. Nineteen over twenty! She'd made the highest grade and had lost no points for two spelling mistakes. There was something she did well! She took the notebook from the teacher, slipped it into her school bag, closed it and mumbled, "Yes, Mademoiselle. Goodbye, Mademoiselle," and remained rooted at the blackboard, her heart thumping inside her.

The teacher asked, "Is there something else?"

Natalie wished she could throw her arms around Mademoiselle Leblanc. But it wouldn't do. Probably right now a couple of the nosiest, meanest girls were in the hall, crawling to the door to hear her punishment for telling lies. Their friends in the cloakroom waited to make fun of her when she came out in tears. She'd show them. She would walk right past them without a word, her head high, to swap her pink overblouse for her jacket.

"Say what's on your mind, Natalie," the teacher said.

"I wanted to say, I just wanted to say thank you."

"It's your work, my child." Mademoiselle smiled. "Off you run."

Natalie sauntered out, finding no one in the corridor. The girls in the cloakroom left as she walked in.

It occurred to her then that Papa was right. Even if the Germans had confiscated her house, she would still have it in her heart and nobody, nobody could take Papa from her. Once home, she would open her Swiss rucksack and take out the magic map with the little markers that Papa had drawn for her. It wasn't just a map about her journey into Switzerland to visit him. Papa made the map to guide her to safety. He was with her then, and he was here now. He would always be with her.

She lifted her jacket from the peg, hung up her overblouse, and shouldered her school bag. She bounced down two flights of stairs, hopping along the hallway to the street, humming the first line of a song she'd just made up. "Thank you! Oh, thank you, Papa!"

Made in the USA
San Bernardino, CA
26 January 2020

63555202R00133